SHADOW OF FEAR

The horses were nervous, uneasy from the scent of blood. Hawk was still hovering over the cowering woman, talking to soothe her. She was calmer now, but the blank staring look in her eyes was not good.

"Her spirit has gone."

It seemed true. The sheer terror of what she had seen had frightened her spirit so badly that it had fled from her body, leaving an empty shell.

"Will it return?" asked Hawk.

"Maybe," Wolf guessed, "maybe not."

They left the campsite behind as the shadows grew long and Sun Boy splashed his paints across the western sky. Maybe it was only coincidence that tonight the splashes were red as blood.

Also by Don Coldsmith

Track
of the
Bear

»»»»»»»»»»»»»»

DON COLDSMITH

BANTAM BOOKS

NEW YORK · TORONTO · LONDON · SYDNEY · AUCKLAND

This edition contains the complete text
of the original hardcover edition.
NOT ONE WORD HAS BEEN OMITTED.

TRACK OF THE BEAR
*A Bantam Book / published by
arrangement with Doubleday*

PUBLISHING HISTORY
*Doubleday edition published May 1994
Bantam edition / January 1995*

*All rights reserved.
Copyright © 1994 by Don Coldsmith.
Cover art copyright © 1994 by Tom Hall.
Library of Congress Catalog Card Number: 93-35514.
No part of this book may be reproduced or transmitted in
any form or by any means, electronic or mechanical,
including photocopying, recording, or by any information
storage and retrieval system, without permission in writing
from the publisher.
For information address:
Doubleday, 1540 Broadway, New York, N.Y. 10036.*

ISBN 0-553-56362-9

Published simultaneously in the United States and Canada

*Bantam Books are published by Bantam Books, a division of
Bantam Doubleday Dell Publishing Group, Inc. Its trademark,
consisting of the words "Bantam Books" and the portrayal of a
rooster, is Registered in U.S. Patent and Trademark Office and
in other countries. Marca Registrada. Bantam Books, 1540
Broadway, New York, New York 10036.*

PRINTED IN THE UNITED STATES OF AMERICA

OPM   0 9 8 7 6 5 4

To the selflessness of those heroes, whatever their faith, who place the well-being of others before their own.

Introduction

»»»

In all cultures there are taboos, laws which are absolute and must never be broken. This is especially true in the tribal religions of Native Americans. There are prescribed results for the willful breaking of such immutable law. Punishment is administered not by the group, but by the spiritual forces of the universe.

The punishment is harsh, usually death. The manner of death may not even be related to the infraction, or to the way in which the law was broken.

Yet, the legends of each nation include stories of those who deliberately broke the laws, fully expecting death. A warrior dying of an incurable illness kills a rattlesnake, which is forbidden in his culture, to hasten his own death. A suicide gesture . . .

More intriguing are the documented cases

in which one is willing to violate the law, sacrificing his own life for what seems a greater good. A holy man may misuse the power of his gift, knowing that such a violation will result in his own death. By dying, he hopes to accomplish one grand triumph which will help his people.

This is a story of a man faced with such a decision.

DON COLDSMITH
1994

Track
of the
Bear

» » » » » » » » » »

1

» » »

It had been a period of good times. The winters had not been unduly harsh for a few seasons. The great buffalo herds had migrated through the Tallgrass Hills, the Sacred Hills of the People. The children were fat and the women were happy, and life was good.

Singing Wolf sat before the lodge, leaning against his willow backrest, smoking and dreaming in the warm autumn sunlight. The Southern band of the People had chosen a good place for winter camp, he thought. There was enough shelter from the strip of oaks along the slope to give some defense against the onslaught of Cold Maker which would come soon. But that was not yet, and though it was the Moon of Madness, the warm days of Second Summer still held.

There seemed no madness at all, except for

the usual antics of the deer that inhabited the timbered strips along the streams. Deer always behave in such a manner as to lend the Moon of Madness its name. It is their rutting season, and the bucks range widely in search of mates, fighting with others they might encounter. The judgment of the animals, too, seems impaired at this time. Only yesterday, a large buck had wandered directly into the camp, oblivious to the danger, its thoughts on romance rather than safety. A couple of youngsters had run for their bows, but in a few moments the buck was gone, leaving the would-be hunters frustrated.

But such is the Moon of Madness. Quail and other birds, flying through the newly leafless thickets, collide with poorly seen twigs and suffer injury or death. It is a cruel way in which the less observant fail to survive, but it is effective. The most alert become the parents of next year's brood.

Humans, too, feel the stresses of the Moon of Madness. It is a frustrated urge to migrate with the high-flying geese, perhaps, or with the slower-moving buffalo. Probably, though, it is only the vague uneasiness as the days become shorter. The Moon of Long Nights lies directly ahead. There is the unspoken dread that Sun Boy's fading torch might go out entirely this time. Such a possibility is enough to make someone a little crazy, is it not?

But the People had prepared well. The storage spaces behind the lodge linings were stuffed with dried meat and pemmican, and with dried corn, beans, and pumpkin obtained in trade from the Growers downstream. Singing Wolf felt secure in the knowledge that the Southern band was ready for winter. This, even though the signs pointed to a hard season. He had conferred on this point with his father, Walks in the Sun. Both agreed, but of course Wolf had learned the intricacies of his station as a holy man from his father. They would be expected to see things alike.

It seemed reasonable, then, that the behavior of the animals in this Moon of Madness might be even more pronounced. Maybe it had begun even earlier, Wolf thought. Now that he recalled, there *had* been a certain restlessness in the buffalo herds that had flowed over the hills like a dark fluid thing that moved and shifted and moved on. And the wolves that had circled the herds, traveling with them and picking off the stragglers, the sick, the old, and the very young, had they already been showing signs of unrest? Possibly. Hindsight is always easier.

There had been one other thing, now that he began to recall. He had noticed more than usual of the great bears that also followed the herds. They were avoided with much care, these grizzled giants, the bear that walks like a man . . . the "real-bear." Far different from the common black bear, these were a source of great wonder as well as a danger in any chance encounter by a hunter.

Horses knew. Their primal instinct gave them fear. Even a faint scent of the hunting bear would make a horse tremble in terror and become unmanageable. The horse knew by the scent that this great beast could kill him as a fox kills a rabbit, and crack his bones as easily.

This knowledge might reach back to the time of Creation, thought Singing Wolf. After all, did not the relationship of the People with the bear go back that far? It was the Covenant, an agreement between the People and Bear, back when the animals could talk, and they and Man all spoke the same tongue. The Covenant provided that the sons of the People would not harm the sons of Bear. They would neither kill them, nor eat of their flesh. In return, Bear's offspring would avoid the People. And it had been so ever since. It was absolutely forbidden for one of the People to harm a bear. *Any* bear. The taboo extended to include the black bear in all of its shades of brown and cinnamon, but also the giant real-bear. To *eat* the flesh of the bear would be virtual cannibalism.

These customs and taboos were not observed by the Head Splitters, allies of the People. But it is often so. Allies need not think or behave exactly alike to have respect for each other. Each has the right to his own ways, and should it not be so? Great Spirit talks to each in his own way, and in the tongue of the listener, so that all may understand.

So the People had little trouble with bears, even the aggressive real-bear who hunted the buffalo. Naturally, confrontation was avoided, but that is only common sense. When even a friend uses an ax, it is wise to stand clear. Likewise, when the bear hunts, it is wise to step aside and give him room.

Singing Wolf was not certain why he was thinking of such things. Later he recognized it as a premonition, but today was too pleasant. Yet, he was observing the behavior of the deer, the quail, the migrating geese. Was there a hint, just a suggestion that there might be a trifle more madness this year in the Moon of Madness?

But all of the signs had been good. And the bears . . . was there really any significance in the fact that there *may* have been more real-bears following the herds this year? *Aiee*, probably not. Some years there are more, or less. It is the same with buffalo, or rabbits, or coyotes. He dismissed it from his mind, and relighted his pipe. It had gone out as he dozed in the warm sun. It was difficult to be deeply concerned over anything on such a day.

His was a good life, he reflected, and he was still young. True, he had realized his gift of the spirit a bit late. First he had become a renowned hunter, one of the first to own and use a thunderstick. Now many of the young men used such weapons, obtained by trading furs to the French. Wolf no longer did much trapping. He had practically discontinued that when he realized that the spirit-gift was more important. Then he had settled down to learn the skills and duties of a holy man from his proud father.

All of this had been ten or twelve summers past. *Aiee*, how time flies! Had he and Rain actually established their own lodge that long ago? It must be, because their children . . . ah, Dawn, so like her mother, would be eleven this year. Three of them; a girl and then two boys, each two years apart. It was good. Dark Antelope, at nine, showed evidence of the athletic ability that had helped earn him his name. Little Owl, now nearing seven seasons, also resembled his namesake. Thoughtful, quiet, and wide-eyed, Little Owl was comical, like a little old man, from the time that he entered the world. He seemed to know all things with an understanding that was almost frightening. Owl seemed to be a favorite of his grandfather, who would spend long times talking to the child, both lost in deep conversation.

Wolf wondered if this quiet, thoughtful child might be the one who would receive the spirit-gift in this generation. Wolf had never spoken of it to Walks in the Sun, but he suspected that he, too, saw this possibility, and perhaps hoped for it. He wondered what the world would be like for these children, with the increasing trade with the French, the broadening range of trade goods, and the growing importance of furs to the whites. *Ah, well,* he thought, *what will be will be.*

His pipe died from neglect again, and he sleepily laid it aside. He did not want to get up to get a brand to relight it, and he could not reach the fire from where he sat. The children were not at hand, and Rain was inside the lodge. *Never mind,* he thought. It was quite comfortable just to sit and drowse.

He may have fallen completely asleep for a moment, he was never sure. He was roused to full alertness by a distant scream. For a moment he interpreted it as a part of his dreamy half-consciousness, but then its significance sank home. It was real. A person in pain and terror had cried out. Could it have been the hunting cry of the cougar, who sometimes sounds like a woman in agony? No, he thought not. This was really a woman.

Rain thrust her head out of the doorway, clearly alarmed.

"What was that?"

"I do not know," he answered. "I—"

He was interrupted by another cry like the first, but this one was cut short, choked off in mid-scream. Wolf jumped to his feet. People were running, calling to each other.

"What is it?"

"It came from that way!"

Men grasped weapons and sprinted in that direction, a timbered gully that slashed the hillside above the camp. The children of Rain and Wolf came running, as they had been taught, and their mother herded them into the lodge.

Singing Wolf was stripping the beaded buckskin case from his musket, checking the flint and the priming as he trotted toward whatever emergency lay out there somewhere.

"Be careful!" called Rain.

Wolf waved and nodded, and moved on, a little faster now. Ahead of him he could hear shouts, and people crashing through the woods. The dead leaves that covered the floor of this little timbered strip magnified every footstep.

What was happening? Could they be under attack? No, this was a more isolated danger, an accident, perhaps. At least, he hoped so. Maybe it would not be serious.

Deep in his heart, he knew better.

2

》》》

The old woman had shuffled along through the crisp fallen leaves, gathering sticks for fuel. She, too, was enjoying the uncommonly fine weather of the late Second Summer. Her search for firewood had taken her somewhat farther from the camp than usual, but it did not matter. It was a good day for such an activity. It would also give her a chance to locate sources of wood for later use. Today was a much more pleasant time to do so than after Cold Maker swept down, graying the sky and chilling the bones with his icy breath.

The band had been camped here for nearly a moon now. Just over the ridge in the next valley was the New band, who had joined the People some ten seasons past. She was not certain that she approved of that, outsiders becoming part of their nation. She had to admit that it had worked well, however. The newcomers were steady and dependable. Their men were good hunters and horsemen, their women hard workers, and their children polite to their elders and well disciplined. It *had* been good to have new stories and new ways of doing things. The strangers had begun to learn the language of the People quickly, so it was no longer necessary to use only hand signs when talking to them. The newcomers had made plain, however, that they intended to keep their own identity. It was a matter of pride with them, probably. That was good. One should have pride in his heritage.

There was talk of giving these newcomers a place in the council, but that was a long way off. As it should be, she thought. Another generation, maybe, if their relationship continued to prosper as it now seemed to do.

She chuckled at herself for filling her head with these deep thoughts of politics on such a lovely day. How had she . . . ? Oh, yes, she had been wondering whether the women of the New band had come this far yet in their search for wood. She must note the best places, gather and store a supply for easy availability near her lodge. It would take more time, more effort, and she was no longer young.

She noticed a small, brushy ravine to her left. Ah! That would be a good source. The trees and bushes, crowding each other for space and sunlight, would produce dead branches. She turned in that direction, breathing a little harder as she struggled up the gentle slope. She paused and looked ahead, and then chuckled with delight. A large tree, once rooted higher up the gully, had toppled into the crevice. Some years before, it appeared, because the tips of the small branches which pointed in her direction were quite dry and brittle. The finest of fuel!

In addition, the venerable old giant had crushed smaller trees as it fell, forming a densely packed windfall of dead wood. Pack-rat nests, as big as her outstretched arms, testified to her first impression that this was a well-seasoned fuel source. And *plentiful*. It would make her winter much easier. She would conceal her discovery. Well, a couple of friends, maybe, to share her good fortune.

For now, she would gather an armful of choice sticks and say nothing. She studied the brushy pile. If she allowed the tips of the nearest branches to remain untouched, they would partially conceal the better fuel inside the crevice. Yes, that would be the way.

Gently, she held a branch aside and stooped as if entering a lodge. She was well into the shadowy space before she became aware of an odor that should not be there. It was not an unpleasant smell, but one which quickly caught her undivided attention.

Man has had much of his sense of smell taken from him since the time of Creation. A gift unused is taken away again, and maybe this is the reason. Mankind, in depending on other senses, sight, hearing, and thought, has perhaps neglected to use the gift of smell as his fellow animals do. In neglect, this important sense has diminished in usefulness.

It is sometimes a surprise, then, when it comes into play again. The slightest hint of a dimly remembered scent can bring back a flood of nearly forgotten memories from childhood. They can be warm and pleasant memories, or may recall bad times. In the case of the old woman, now well inside the windfall, it was neither. It was merely a recognition, but one which caused every hair on her body to prickle, and which struck terror in her heart. The warm animal scent, now heavy in the stale air of the crevice, was one she had experienced only once before, many winters past. It was the smell of a newly abandoned bear's den, shown to her by her father when she was a child.

This was the same scent, but with a subtle difference. Perhaps it was her nose, or maybe some unknown instinct that told her the difference. But it was plain. The bear's lodge so long ago had been empty, abandoned. This time, the warm animal smell told her instantly that this was not an abandoned den. Its occupant was still using this lodge, and a cold sweat broke out on her skin as she realized that it was probably here now, at this very moment.

The animal should be asleep, having started its winter hibernation, but with the unusual weather . . . Very slowly and carefully she began to make her way back out through the tangle of branches. Why did it seem that there were so many more now to impede her retreat? Or that her moccasined feet were creating so much more noise? Her fear rose, her body damp with the sweat of terror. Its scent mingled with the heavy animal smells of the den.

A little farther now . . . a few more steps . . . trying not to break a stick underfoot. The rustling of the dry leaves beneath her moccasins was like a rushing of the wind, and there was a roaring in her ears. And now the roar was real. It filled the crevice, reverberating with a tremor that shook her frail bones to the marrow.

She broke into the open, brushing the last few branches aside as she broke free. The noise behind her, the rustling and the crash of breaking branches, mingled with the deep growling roar, caused her to turn and look back into the dusky crevice.

It would have made no difference had she continued to flee without looking. Another step or two . . . The head of the creature as it burst into the light seemed as broad as her own body. It was little more than an arm's length away, the wide forehead, dark little eyes, and the great snarling mouth with its gleaming teeth. And not the black bear she had expected, but the great grizzled real-bear. It made little difference now, but it was somehow more horrible. She screamed and turned to run, but her stiff old limbs refused to obey. She slipped and fell heavily, and rolled to look again at her attacker.

Now the creature rose to its hind legs, seeming to grow as it did so. So tall . . . twice her own height, even had she been standing. It moved toward her, and she screamed again with her last breath as the bear dropped to all fours to attack.

The first of the would-be rescuers saw the bear tearing at the frail body, shaking it as a dog shakes a rat. It was torn and broken, and already there was little that still resembled the appearance of poor Corn Woman.

They stopped, watching. What could be done? The Covenant with Bear prohibited their shooting at the creature. But more men were now arriving, and there were shouts and yells.

"What is it? An enemy? An attack?"

"No. A bear . . . it has killed Corn Woman."

"*Aiee! A bear?*"

"Yes . . . look!"

As the noise and confusion grew, the bear became alarmed. Dropping the broken corpse, it stood erect again and roared its challenge. There was a gasp at its size, its head towering among the trees. Even though it was nearly a bow shot away, its appearance was one to strike terror to the hearts of the most fearless hunters. Some prepared to flee if necessary.

"Remember our Covenant, brother Bear," someone said softly.

There was no reaction from the other men. The remark was a serious prayer, and recognized as such.

But now the bear was becoming more restless. It roared once more, then dropped to all fours and moved at a deliberate pace away from the startled warriors. It was at this moment that Singing Wolf arrived, puffing a little from the exertion. The scene needed no explanation.

"*Aiee!*" Wolf said softly. "The real-bear. He has killed?"

"Yes. Corn Woman, we think. See, next to the tree there?"

Wolf nodded. The bear was moving on

now, and had disappeared from sight in the timber along the river.

"Let us care for her body," said a man, his voice tight. "Someone must tell her husband, too."

"I will tell him, and bring a robe to wrap her," volunteered another. "He is my uncle."

It was a quiet and subdued group that cautiously approached the still form in the trees. They were cautious, ready to flee if the bear returned. The wail of the Mourning Song rose from the camp, and they knew that the old man had been told of his loss.

The young relative returned with a nearly new buffalo robe. They gently lifted the slender remains to its surface, arranging the limbs as best they could, wrapping for the burial ceremony.

"Tell us, holy man," someone asked Singing Wolf. "Why did Bear break his Covenant with the People?"

Singing Wolf was at a loss to answer. In his lifetime there had never been such an occurrence.

"I do not know," he admitted. "My father, though, may understand."

There were nods of assent. One must have respect for age and experience in a holy man. It was also noted, however, that one must respect a holy man who can gracefully admit that he does not know. Singing Wolf lost nothing in stature that day.

It was night before the meeting around the fire by the lodge of Walks in the Sun. Most of the important men of the band were there, their robes drawn around them in the chill of the autumn. They smoked and visited, but everyone was waiting for the words of the old holy man. Walks in the Sun had traveled far and seen much. His words would be respected.

The pipe finished its rounds and the holy man cleared his throat. There was an expectant silence.

"I have been asked," he began, "how it is that Bear has broken the Covenant."

Many nodded in agreement.

"Tell me," he went on, "what the trackers found."

Walks in the Sun had not gone to the scene of the attack. Now, one of the most respected of trackers among the People prepared to answer. He was called Sees, because his full name, Sees Where There Is Little to See, was too cumbersome.

"Yes," Sees related, "I have studied this place. I am made to think that our sister, Corn Woman, was gathering wood. Her sticks were scattered by the windfall. But she may have been inside, among the branches of the big oak.

There were sticks there. The bear should have been in winter sleep, but it is warm yet. Maybe he was not. Or not deeply asleep. If Corn Woman woke him . . . Well, I think that is what happened. One other thing . . . there was one very clear track where the bear walked away. My brothers, I have seen many tracks, over many years. But never the track of a real-bear as big as this."

He fell silent, and there was a murmur of apprehension. Walks in the Sun held up a hand, and the circle quieted.

"Now," said the holy man, "what would you do if someone forced his way into your lodge and woke you from sleep?"

There were puzzled looks. What did this . . . ?

"Kill him!" said a young man.

There was laughter, and a more moderate voice spoke.

"Prepare to defend youself."

"Yes," agreed the holy man. "Now, is this not what Bear would do? And is Bear not as grumpy about his winter sleep as our young friend here?"

Again, laughter at the expense of the young hothead.

"But look," Walks in the Sun went on, "if you were Bear, and Corn Woman came into your winter lodge . . ."

There were now nods of understanding, though still a few puzzled looks.

"I am made to think," he continued, "that Bear would believe the Covenant was broken by Corn Woman. It is hard to accept for her husband, but my brothers, such things happen. Who has not had a misunderstanding in his own lodge?"

Chuckles indicated that this was a principle that could be easily understood. The holy man continued.

"If it is that easy for those who share a lodge to have a misunderstanding, how much easier between us and Bear? No, I am made to think that it was not Bear who broke the agreement, but Mankind, in the form of Corn Woman. It is too bad . . . a tragedy, but it has happened before. Such is the world. This reminds us again of our Covenant."

The circle began to break up, as people sought their own lodges. It would be uncomfortably cold tonight. Besides, there was a chill over the camp of the People that could not quite be dispelled by the interpretation given by Walks in the Sun.

3

»»»

Singing Wolf, by light of day the next morning, realized that his father was probably right. An old woman, blundering into the den of a real-bear, should expect the worst. It had happened. There was really no mystery, was there? He tried to shrug it off.

The continued wail of the Song of Mourning rose and fell across the camp as her husband and family mourned the loss of Corn Woman. It bothered Wolf, for this was something that should not have been. Mourning was not unusual among the People. Their way of life was full of danger, a fall from a horse, an accident in the hunt. Sometimes, even, a skirmish with another tribe. Such deaths were times of sadness, but after the prescribed period of three days' mourning the People would return to the ways of the living. After all, is dying not merely a part of living?

This was not what whispered in the dark recesses of the young man's mind. These things, the dying, mourning, the crossing over of the spirit, were all a part of the way of things. They were expected as a risk of being alive. One would have no such risks unless he was alive, no?

He even tried to convince himself that this death was less important because of the age and infirmity of Corn Woman. It was not unusual in the legends of the People for such a person to end his own life, or hers, for the greater good. In times of starvation, an aging warrior might walk off into a raging blizzard, proudly singing the Death Song. It was a challenge to the enemy, Cold Maker, as he might have challenged a human enemy in his youth. A resolve to die, so that there would be more of the scant food supply left for the children. A noble death. A choice.

> *The grass and the sky go on*
> *forever,*
> *But today is a good day to*
> *die . . .*

He could not persuade himself that this death was of that sort. Times were not hard, there was no starvation. As far as he knew, Corn Woman had not been sad or morose. But this was not the action of one whose life was good.

Still deep in thought, Wolf went to talk to the bereaved husband. Maybe he could find some answer there. He approached the lodge and paused awkwardly before the wailing figure seated in the doorway.

"My heart is heavy for you, Uncle," he said.

The old man paused to nod in appreciation of the visit, but it was plain that this was not a time for conversation. Singing Wolf paused only long enough to speak briefly to the other mourners, the sons and daughters of the dead woman. Then he hurried on.

He had assured himself of one thing. This death had been totally unexpected, and had not been a matter of choice by the victim. The gnawing doubt remained in his mind. The whole thing seemed clear-cut, but *what if . . . ?* He could not shake the thought that there was a difference here. Had there been something about the bear? He could not remember that anyone had ever blundered into the den of a real-bear, or even found one. Could it have been a spirit-bear, one not of this world? There were old legends of such things, but the coming alive of evil spirits in a manner such as this was not a major part of the lore of the People.

No, Wolf told himself for the hundredth time. It was only a natural thing, an accident, though a very unusual one. But he kept remembering the question that had been raised at the time of Corn Woman's death. Why did Bear break the Covenant?

The obvious answer, given through the wisdom of Walks in the Sun, was that Bear had *not*. The People seemed to accept it well, and in his mind, Wolf did also. In his heart, it was not so easy. The suspicion lingered that there was something here that was not quite right. Something deeper and more important to the People than the mere death of an old woman in an accident. He tried to put it aside.

The winter came on with a vengeance in the Moon of Long Nights. Cold Maker roared across the plains and howled through the timbered strips along the watercourses. The People retreated to their lodges, built windbreaks of brush, and piled snow around the base of the lodge skins. They sometimes glanced anxiously at dwindling supplies of firewood, but on every possible day they gathered more.

There was one source of fuel, however, that no one approached. The great pile of dry wood in the windfall was avoided as if it were forbidden. No one wished to find out if the great bear still wintered there. The general feeling among the experienced hunters and trappers was that the bear was gone. It had not been seen since that day, the day of Corn Woman's death. Probably it had traveled far and rapidly after all the shouting and excitement. The warm weather had held for a few days, and no doubt the bear had spent that time looking for a better place to spend its winter sleep.

Conversations with members of the New band had revealed that they had seen nothing of the creature. They had no special reverence for Bear, though, it seemed. They even hunted the black bear on occasion. Similarly, they usually avoided the real-bear because of the danger involved in its unpredictable nature and its aggressiveness.

"They are much like the Head Splitters in this, then?" asked Walks in the Sun.

Wolf had told him of a conversation with a holy man of the New band.

"Yes, it seems so, Father. Like us, they would rather eat buffalo, but they have nothing against eating bear meat."

"It is strange, is it not," the old man mused, "how Great Spirit has spoken to each group in different ways."

"Are you made to think," asked Wolf, "that it is all one Spirit?"

The eyes of Walks in the Sun twinkled in amusement.

"I am made to think," he observed, "that I do not know. Those of our New band speak of 'Man Above.' He is the Great Spirit who speaks with their tongue. But would not such a powerful spirit speak *all* tongues, each to his own?"

Wolf nodded thoughtfully. "But is it the *same* Spirit, Father?"

The old man was staring at the fire, smoking and lost in thought. Now he pointed at the curling flames.

"Is that the same fire," he asked with a smile, "that now dwells in my pipe? Or the one in the cooking fire of Dog Woman's lodge over there?"

Wolf shrugged. He knew that this was not really a question. His father was about to make a point.

"I do not understand fire," Walks in the Sun went on, "but I use it. It is so with things of the spirit. We do not have to understand, only to enjoy."

The question Wolf had originally raised still hung unanswered, and he started to speak. His father held up a hand to stop him.

"An ancestor of ours," the old man continued, "once said that there are many paths up the sides of the hill, but they all go to the top of the hill. Maybe it is like that."

Wolf made one more try. "I do not under-stand—"

"Wolf," his father interrupted, "if you still think you have to understand, you have missed the message. Relax, *let* it happen. You still try sometimes to *make* it happen. Your guide will help you."

The younger man was still troubled. He was still a novice in the ways of a holy man, he thought.

"What if I use it wrong, because I do not know?" he had once asked his father.

Walks in the Sun's answer had been quick. "Your guide will not let you!"

Wolf thought of that now, as his father continued.

"Wait, be patient, my son. And above all, *listen*. Listen to what your guide tells you. Your understanding is good, Wolf. But some-times you try too hard." He smiled affection-ately. "Your guide tried for a long time to get your attention. Now, listen. The answers to your questions will come, but listen for your guide."

The old man rose, indicating that the con-versation was at an end.

Wolf was still uneasy, and did not under-stand why. What if his spirit-guide was trying to get his attention and he was not recognizing it? Was that the cause of his uneasiness? It was a frustrating situation. Somehow, Wolf was certain that there was something more. They had not heard the last of the bear.

There was nothing to do about it, of course. The season went on, despite such doubts. The odd and isolated incident of the bear had been set aside by most of the People as a single event with no real connection to anything else. It would go down in the legends of the People as the odd year when, in the Moon of Madness, Corn Woman was killed by a bear.

And that was the idea that had become unacceptable to young Singing Wolf. Deep in his heart, he was convinced that the event of this strange season was only a beginning of strange events to come. Well, his father was right on one score. He must wait, because bears and the People alike would be huddled in their lodges until the Moon of Awakening.

When it did come, the news was not of a particularly exciting nature. It was late in the Moon of Hunger, just before the Moon of Awakening. A few warm days, a slight thaw, and the shoots of green began to appear in sheltered places. Pockets of snow on the wooded slopes began to melt and trickle in tiny rivulets, joining together in larger streams to run toward the river.

Geese were seen, moving high in the blue of the renewed sky. Yellow-green buds on the willows gave promise of new leaves to come soon. The world was good.

There was the smell of awakening, and the People began to come out and move around. Children threw snowballs of the melting snow, and it now seemed that once more, Sun Boy had renewed his torch and turned back Cold Maker for the season.

A trio of young men from the camp of the New band came over to visit, exchange stories and smokes, and inquire about the winter's experiences. It was the way of things. After a period of restriction, it seems important to see and talk to different people.

They spoke to Singing Wolf of some trapping they had done, between the worst of the storms. The otter had been good, the beaver fair. Weather had been the hardest part.

"Now it is over for the season," they observed a little sadly. "The fur will soon be shedding."

Wolf nodded. "Will you go to trade soon?" he asked.

"Probably. Maybe a few of us will go, and then meet our people at the Sun Dance."

Already, Wolf noted, the New people were

planning their season around the Sun Dance. They were rapidly becoming a part of the People.

"It is good," he told them. "How soon will you go?"

"Depends on the weather."

There was no urgency. Besides, Sun Boy and Cold Maker would have a few more skirmishes, perhaps ugly ones. It would not be good to be traveling then.

They finished the pipes, and the visitors rose to leave. Then one turned back.

"Oh, yes, we nearly forgot. We saw the tracks of your real-bear."

Instantly, Wolf was alert.

"Where?"

"Beyond the ridge. *Aiee*, this is a big one! I never saw bigger tracks!"

Wolf had begun to think of the great bear at less frequent intervals in the recent past. There were other distractions, and the season was not conducive to thoughts of bears, who were hibernating anyway.

Now it all came crashing back into his mind. Maybe he had forced himself to set such thoughts aside, but he could do so no longer. He had no idea where the bear had wintered. It did not matter. It had returned. Once more Wolf had the odd premonition that this was no ordinary situation. Even a real-bear . . . No, there was something about this that made his neck hairs prickle and filled him with dread. This was a terrible shadow of some sort over the lives of the People.

4

》》 》》 》》

Despite Wolf's misgivings, there was no further problem with the bear that spring. The Moon of Awakening turned to that of Greening, and the People became restless to travel.

A trade party made up of men from the Southern band and the New band put together a pack train of furs and departed to trade with the French. Those left behind would move in a northwesterly direction at a more leisurely pace, planning to arrive at the Sun Dance site in the Moon of Roses. That was two moons away, but they would hunt as they traveled. At some point they should begin to encounter buffalo as the herds moved northward for the season.

Maybe it would be a good year to burn the grass, thought Wolf. That would bring the herds into the burned area. He discussed the possibilities with his father.

"Let us wait and see," suggested the older man. "We have food for now. It is not needed to burn every year. But you are right. If we do, it should be soon. I will cast the bones."

The bones indicated mostly good fortune, and it was decided not to burn. There were buffalo in the area, and a few good kills were all that were needed.

Probably, Wolf decided, the bear that had so occupied his thoughts had moved on, with plenty of food available. With the warming weather and the optimism of springtime, it was hard for him to think of how gloomy he had become over the incident of the bear. Maybe his dire feeling of doom was wrong. Possibly he had overreacted to the sight of the broken body of poor old Corn Woman.

Well, the bear was gone now. It had quite possibly been one that migrated with the herds, had selected this area for its winter sleep, and was now gone with the moving geese. It might be many sleeps north by this time, circling some distant buffalo herd, looking for the sick, the weak, and the young. Yes, his father had probably been right all along. It was just an accident.

The People struck the big lodges and moved out late in the Moon of Growing. The weather was good, and travel easy. Their scouts, or "wolves," circled the caravan constantly, looking for any potential danger, though none was expected. The season was past when there would be danger in a prairie fire. The dead stalks of last year's grass were matting down, damp and decaying, a nutrient mulch for this year's new growth. There were few enemies, if any. In reality, one of the main functions of the advance wolves was to choose the route of travel. It was no small task to transport the heavily laden pole-drags . . . *travois*, the French traders now called them. Some places were so rough that though the horse could easily travel, the *travois* could not follow.

Occasionally the column would be routed around a band of grazing buffalo. Or perhaps there would be a short rest stop while the People's wolves chased a few animals clear of their intended route. It could be quite dangerous if a stray animal or two attempted to rejoin the herd on the other side of the straggling column.

All of this happened, of course, as a matter of habit, practically without even thinking about it. And when the wolves selected the camp site for the night stop, the routine was quite simple. Each family selected its place, marked it with a pile of their belongings, and started a fire. The fire is a ritual in all cultures. It announces one's presence, establishes evidence of his existence, and of his intention to be there, at least for the present.

For the People, it was also an effort to contact the spirits of a new place, requesting their good will by offering a pinch of tobacco in the first curling flames of a new fire.

Here I camp tonight, this is my place for now. Accept my small gift in thanks for a safe camp.

Unless it appeared that a major storm was likely, the lodges would not be erected. It was too great a task to set up the poles and lift the heavy skin cover into place for the short time that they would be there. If any shelter at all was needed, or desired for privacy, it would be a simple screen of willow branches. At most, an open-sided lean-to.

Sometimes the children of two or more families would set up their own "camp" near that of the parents, building their own small shelters. It was good to do so, and furnished a chance to learn by one's mistakes without penalty, as they mimicked the work of their elders.

So, the travel went well, and there was no incident for the first six or seven sleeps. Then came the incident which made it quite plain that it was not to be an easy summer. Even then, no one recognized yet . . .

*　　*　　*

The young couple had slipped away to spend some time in private courting. They were childhood sweethearts, friends during their years in the Rabbit Society as they grew up. Songbird had reached maturity first, as women do, changing her shape and adding a graceful willowy sway to her way of walking. Her long legs, previously thin and round like sticks, had become well shaped, with seductive swelling of the calves and contrasting slenderness in the ankles. The women of the People were proud of their legs and of their beauty in general. It had been a thrill to the girl to note her enlarging breasts begin to feel confined in the softness of her buckskin dress.

She had been glad, a year later, when Lost Horse had made his move to maturity. She had teased him a little, but both understood, because they were friends. His muscled arms and shoulders began to broaden. His voice changed, and there now grew a thin fringe of fur across his upper lip and along his jaw line. Soon he would begin to pluck these hairs, but for now it was something to display with a degree of pride. Songbird teased him about this, too.

"When are you going to make yourself presentable?"

"When I am ready," he would growl with his newly resonant voice, reveling in its deep tones.

On this evening they had strolled out of the camp, nodding to the sentry as they passed, and made their way to a rocky little glen across the stream. It was little more than a bowshot away from the hustle and bustle of the camp, but it was private. They had found little privacy since the journey started, and it was precious to them. They would probably ask their parents' permission to marry soon . . . maybe at the Sun Dance.

It was nearly twilight, a warm evening, and it was pleasant to sit together on a sun-warmed rock. They listened to the gentle buzz of activity across the stream, talked and laughed together, and it was good.

They embraced, and as she turned her head, Songbird caught a hint of motion at the corner of her vision. She jumped, startled, and gasped at the shadowy figure rising from the rocks behind Lost Horse. At first she thought that someone had followed them. Her younger brother and some of his friends, maybe. Her anger rose, but changed to fear as the manlike figure rose, standing and towering over them. She could actually smell the creature now, and it growled a guttural grinding sound that grew into a roar.

By that time she was screaming, pushing her companion away and rolling clear.

"Run!" she yelled, and the two of them

dashed for the stream, with the great bear in hot pursuit. It dropped to all fours, barely a pace behind them as they clattered across the gravel bar.

Then, not really by design, the two young people parted, making their way separately, a space of a step or two between them. This seemed to confuse their pursuer for a moment. The animal darted first at one, then the other, wasting time in indecision while they made their escape.

"What is it?" called the sentry.

"The bear!" Songbird screamed.

Now they were nearing the first of the fires, and the sentry was retreating with them. People were running, shouting, and in all the confusion the two lovers now realized that they were no longer pursued. It had been a narrow escape.

Everyone was talking at once, bubbling with excitement, but no one was eager to leave the comparative safety of the fires.

The People slept little that night, and when the sun rose, a party of warriors cautiously crossed the stream to look around. Sees, the tracker, went ahead to look for sign, and returned to the others with a puzzled look.

"There is nothing," he told them. "No tracks at all."

There was a general discussion while they

prepared to break camp. It must be noted, some argued, that the rocky glen was not a good place for tracks. Most of the pursuit was across gravel and shallow water. And even Sees was not overwhelmingly interested in challenging a real-bear in its own territory. He would look quickly and retreat. The tracker could not be criticized for that. It was only sensible.

Basically, the primary goal now was to break camp and leave the area as quickly as possible. If there was a bear, so be it. They would leave its territory, as the Covenant dictated, and leave the risk behind.

In a half-day's travel the fears of the night seemed to have dissolved. It was hard to think dark thoughts of marauding real-bears with the sun shining brightly and travel going well.

There developed a strange reaction on the part of the fun-loving band. After all, no one had actually seen the bear except the two young lovers. They had said that it growled and roared, but the sentry had heard only the girl's scream. They began to joke and tease about the incident.

"She probably saw Horse and thought he was a bear," an old woman laughed. "He *is* getting hairy-faced!"

"Yes . . . Then she screamed and Horse thought it was a bear's roar."

The joking continued, the interpretations becoming more and more absurd.

"They chased each other across the stream."

The sentry did not help matters by reminding that he had seen no bear.

To Songbird and Lost Horse, it was not funny at all. They sought out Walks in the Sun.

"Uncle," Horse began hesitantly, "we would talk with you."

"Yes?"

"Uncle, you have heard the jokes about our escape last night."

The holy man nodded.

"But there *was* a bear!" the girl blurted.

He studied the two for a little while before he spoke.

"Yes," he said quietly. "I am made to think so."

"Then why were there no tracks?"

He shrugged.

"Of that I am not sure. Maybe there were tracks, but Sees did not find them. He looked only for a short time, you know."

"But we *did* see it, Uncle."

"Yes. But let them have their fun. They know that the tracker searched for only a short while. There was hardly a chance to find tracks. He knows that he might have missed them."

Reluctantly, they turned to leave. Singing Wolf had overheard the conversation as he adjusted his saddle cinch.

"Do you think that, Father?" he asked.

"Of course," answered Walks in the Sun. "Unless . . ."

"Unless what?" Wolf felt a chill creeping up his spine. His father had, all along, insisted that the death of Corn Woman and the entire matter of the real-bear were not really unusual events. Was he now changing his ideas?

"Unless," the holy man said quietly, "it is a bear who does not leave tracks."

5

» » »

A *spirit-bear?* One that would not leave tracks?

Earlier, Walks in the Sun had been completely unwilling to consider such an explanation. When Wolf had mentioned it, his father had dismissed the idea quickly. The older man had insisted that the killing of Corn Woman held no real significance. A perfectly understandable event, the woman was in the wrong place at the wrong time. That was all.

Now there had been this odd conversation between the two, in which his father kept nudging Wolf to look and listen for the spirit-side, the mystical. That was always an important aspect of the holy man's career. Maybe the most important. But why had Walks in the Sun been so sure that the incident of the bear's kill was *not* a spirit-thing, and was now suggesting that it might be?

Wolf's father had never been one to waver. He did sometimes change his way of thinking, however. Maybe he had been trying to suggest a change, without being too obvious. Or perhaps he was only trying to force his son into considering all possibilities. He had done that before, during the period of apprenticeship. And actually, was a holy man's apprenticeship ever finished? One should still be learning all of his life, and probably beyond, on the Other Side.

Yes, now that he thought of their conversation, Wolf became convinced that its purpose was to urge that he consider all possibilities, and be willing to change his thinking, if necessary. How clever of his father, to suggest and then let his student wrestle with it.

Well, Wolf thought, *I have wrestled with it all winter*. But now, with a new occurrence, he must review again the events with the bear.

There had been three, not counting the fact that there had seemed to be more realbears following the herds last season. Maybe that in itself was significant, and must be considered. Maybe the bears intended to move into the Sacred Hills of the People and claim the territory for bears. An odd thought, but it must be kept in mind. Various birds and animals sometimes changed their range. He set that idea aside for further thought later.

The first real event had been Corn Woman's death. There was plenty of physical sign there. A number of people had seen the bear as it fled. No, it did not really flee, it had been said. The creature retreated, but with dignity and pride. And it had left tracks. There had been much comment about their length, and the immense size of the bear. So far, it seemed a purely understandable situation.

Why, then, had he had such a feeling that it was *not?*

His thoughts moved on. The next sign of the bear had been in the spring, when it came out of winter sleep. That too had been a perfectly normal thing. The New band across the ridge had seen tracks. *Only* tracks, in the mud and melting snow of the Awakening. So be it. Bears come out of their winter lodges and move around at that time. But it had not even been seen. There was one other thing, though. There seemed no doubt that this was the *same* bear, a fact suggested by the immense size of its tracks.

Again, *tracks.* And after these two events, there was still no suggestion that this was anything more than a large real-bear, with slightly strange behavior. Nothing, that is, except the still, small warning voice in the back of Wolf's mind.

This third event had been different. But

had it, really? A young couple had been badly frightened in the long shadows of evening by a great bear. They were probably very fortunate to have escaped at all. Yet there was the persistent story that there had not been a bear, that the shadows had deceived them. Wolf did not think so. He knew these young people, had talked to them soon after the event. He was convinced that they had seen a bear.

Then why were there no tracks? Wolf went to the area the next morning before the People moved out. He did not want to go too far into the rocky glen, but he did poke around the gravel bar. It was trampled and disturbed by many feet now, and he could tell nothing. *But I am not a tracker*, he thought. And there was the nagging impression that he was being watched. He was very uncomfortable there, and soon retreated.

On the way back to the camp that they would soon leave, a thought occurred to him. He would go and talk to the tracker. He found Sees loading his family's *travois* for the day's travel.

"May I speak with you, Uncle?"

Sees nodded, and Wolf noted in passing that the man appeared uncomfortable, ill at ease.

"I would ask," began Wolf. "You saw no tracks at the stream?"

"None," grunted the tracker.

"How is it, Uncle, that such a great creature leaves no tracks?" asked Wolf.

Sees waited a moment before answering, and then chose his words very carefully.

"I did not say there were no tracks. I said I saw none."

"But . . . you are . . ."

"Yes, I am a tracker. I did not want to follow into unknown places."

The dread in the man's voice was unexpected. Sees had a reputation that said he was afraid of nothing. Could he, too, have a strange feeling about this?

"That is wise," agreed Wolf, "but I wondered. Do you think this bear might be different?"

There was a flash of surprise on the tracker's face, but only for a moment. He regained his composure.

"How?" he asked.

Wolf shrugged. "I do not know. I felt that it may be."

Sees stared at him for a moment, appearing undecided.

"Wolf," he said finally, "you are the holy man, who understands such things."

Ah! thought Wolf. *He does suspect something unusual!* Sees would not imply that this was a matter for a holy man unless he suspected something of the spirit.

"There are many things that I do not understand, Uncle," Wolf said cautiously. "Why does a bear leave tracks sometimes and sometimes not?"

Now the tracker seemed uneasy again. "I did not say there were no tracks," he repeated. "Wolf, I must finish packing."

He turned away.

"Wait!" said Wolf. "One more thing. I felt, this morning, that I was watched, there by the stream. Did you, too, feel this?"

Sees turned, and there was a startled look on his face. He was pale.

"You, too?" he asked, hardly louder than a whisper.

Wolf nodded. It was good to know that someone else was having these disturbing thoughts too. But now was not a time to push it further.

"We will speak of it later," he promised.

He turned back toward his own lodge, where he helped Rain with the heavy part of the loading. They paused to rest a moment as they watched the final preparations of neighboring families, waiting to depart.

"What is it, Wolf?" asked his wife.

"What . . . ? Did you speak?" he muttered.

"Yes. I asked what is the matter. You are a long way off this morning."

"I am sorry, Rain. The thing of the bear last night."

"Yes, that was a worrisome thing. They were very lucky, no?"

He nodded. Rain did not understand the depth of his concern. He had not discussed it with her, because it was something so ethereal that it could not be put into words. What can be discussed about a *feeling!* Yet, he had always told her of his thoughts and fears.

"Rain," he said seriously, "you know there were no tracks there at the stream last night?"

She looked surprised, but interested.

"I thought they did not look very hard." She smiled. "*I* would have spent very little time there."

"I, too," he agreed. "But Rain, I am made to think that this is a very strange thing."

"What? That they found no tracks?"

"Yes . . . well, no. That is part of it. I do not know. It is only that I have this feeling. This bear is more important than the People think."

"Ah, I know your feelings!" she exclaimed. "You think this is a thing of the spirit!"

He was startled for a moment, but not really. They had been so close for so long, since childhood, really. Every thought of either of them was usually known to the other. Rain's eyes widened now.

"This has bothered you since the death of the woman!"

She did not speak the name of the dead woman. One does not speak the name of the dead, unless someone else also bears that name. Probably there were others, but if in doubt . . . It is easier to avoid such a risk anyway.

"I . . . maybe so," he agreed. "Rain, my heart is heavy over this, because I do not know."

"What does your father say?"

"That is part of it. He first said no, it is not a spirit-animal. Now he seems to think 'maybe.' "

"Because of no tracks?"

"He did not say so very strongly, but he mentioned it."

"And you?" she asked.

"At first I felt there was something very strange . . . spirit-like. Then, when my father said no, and no one else thought so, I thought no, it must not be so."

"Until now?"

"Yes. Rain, I talked to Sees this morning. I am made to think that he feels this dark threat to the People too."

"Aiee! He said so?"

"Almost. We are to talk again."

Rain sat, lost in thought. When she finally spoke, it was slowly and thoughtfully.

"You are puzzled at a creature that sometimes leaves tracks and sometimes not?"

"Well, yes. That is one thing."

Rain nodded. "Now," she went on, "a normal bear should leave tracks all the time, no?"

"But maybe it did, and Sees just did not find them," Wolf protested.

"True. But a spirit-bear could leave them or not, *as it chose?*"

The chill at the back of his neck became colder.

"Yes . . . I suppose."

Rain laughed nervously. "So it is either a spirit-bear, or Sees is not as good as he used to be?"

"He is very skilled, Rain. And he feels something . . ."

They looked into each other's eyes and realized the conclusion that they were approaching.

"Then . . ." Rain began.

"No, do not say it. Let us still say maybe." Wolf urged. "And maybe we will leave it behind, here."

A long shout signaled that the column was

ready to move out. They called to the children, and Wolf mounted his horse. He took a long look at the dark glen beyond the stream. *No*, he thought, *whatever it is, we will not leave it here.*

6

>> >> >>

It had helped him considerably to talk with Rain. The mere fact that someone else knew of his doubts was helpful. He looked forward to talking at greater length with Sees about his feelings. What did the tracker feel? He also wanted to discuss further with his father. If there seemed a possibility of a spirit-animal, was there any way to predict its behavior? Could it change back and forth as it wished, coming and going to the spirit-world and back?

Maybe, he thought, the narrow escape of the young lovers was due to the fact that the creature was in the process of changing over, and was mostly spirit. But how long would such a change take, and would it be *more* dangerous in spirit-form, or less? *Aiee*, he longed to go back to the time when he did not have such a problem.

Then he smiled to himself. Had there ever been a time without a problem? Probably not. There had even been a time when he had thought that Rain was about to marry a handsome young man from the Eastern band. It was amusing now, but at the time his heart had been heavy. It had not helped that his friend Fast Turtle kept teasing him. Being bested by a man from the Eastern band, who were noted for foolishness, was a great disgrace, and Turtle had not let him forget. It had all turned out well, and Rain came back to him.

It would be good to see Fast Turtle again at the Sun Dance. Turtle had married into the Mountain band, and was living with them. Wolf wondered whether he could explain his thoughts to Fast Turtle, who had never seemed to have a serious thought in his life. Probably not. Turtle was a perpetual youngster, never quite overcoming his love for jokes and adolescent behavior. But he was still a friend, and it would be good to see him.

Anyway, he could look forward to the excitement of the Sun Dance. It was exhausting, the endless days of ceremonial ritual and dance. There were great responsibilities for the holy men, too. But there were the few days before and after the formal ceremonies, when the People threw themselves into the joy of the season. Reunion with friends and relatives,

the contests and games and races, mock battles
between the young men. Courtships renewed,
continued, or newly begun. The Big Council
was always exciting, with the leaders and sub-
chiefs of each band recounting the events of
the year to the others.

Above all, though, the Sun Dance itself.
What a filling of the heart, to celebrate the return of the sun, the grass, and the buffalo. And
aside from the main theme, the private demon-
strations of thanksgiving, patriotism, and sup-
plication. Sacrifices before the effigy of the
great bull buffalo in the open-sided medicine
lodge. There would be vows made and vows
fulfilled, and the People would be whole again.

The Southern band would have much to
recount in the Big Council this year. Maybe the
Council would include discussion that might
prove enlightening on the subject of the spirit-
bear. Like it or not, and with no further evidence, that was the term used more and more
frequently by the People of the Southern band.

There had been several more scares by the
time they approached the appointed meeting
place for the Sun Dance. A woman gathering
buffalo chips for her evening fire had heard
noises and had seen the willows moving along
the stream. She dropped her fuel and fled.

Children frightened each other by tales of
the spirit-bear, and by hiding and leaping out

with a growling roar. Such play eventually sub-
sided, forbidden by most parents. The adults
were uneasy enough without such foolishness.

But there were other things, ill-defined
events that were more impressive in their nature. A sentry, watching outside the camp one
night as they traveled, had seen things for
which he could not find answers. He had
shared his experience with Singing Wolf, who
was a boyhood friend. There was really not
much to tell. At least, nothing that was definite enough to notify others.

It had been an odd, changeable night, with
a bright moon. But a weather change was in the
making, and patches of fast-moving clouds
were scudding across the sky. The general effect was that of shifting patterns of light and
shadow across the prairie. It had appeared that
the surface of the earth itself was alive, writh-
ing and squirming as the shadows slipped and
rolled over the distant hills. Nearer, tiny scraps
of shadow would seem to race at an obstacle,
such as a clump of willows, and slither *over* the
top to sprawl on the flat meadow beyond.
Hawk was rather enjoying the experience,
when he noticed that one shadow was moving
in a different direction from the rest. The
breeze high above the surface, which seemed to
be driving the hurrying clouds, was from the
west. This was normal for the season, during a

weather change. But one shadow, perhaps a bowshot away, was moving *upwind*, against the motion of the rest.

He was startled, and tried to watch it. That itself was difficult. The patch of darkness seemed to move of its own volition, wandering independently of the other shades. More alarming yet, it appeared to change shape constantly, growing taller or broader as it moved. He watched, cold sweat popping out on his skin, as once it seemed to move directly toward him for a moment or two. He nearly fled to give the alarm, but the apparition turned and flowed the other way.

Hawk was glad later that he had not sounded an alarm. He would have been teased forever for rousing the People for a shadow. He did become quite uneasy a little later when a larger cloud blackened the entire area in front of him for a little while. When it passed, the prairie was silvered with moonlight again, and the aberrant shadow was nowhere to be seen. Still, it was with great relief that he saw the yellowing of the false dawn as the sky began to pale in the east. He hurried to find his friend the holy man.

"It was nothing I could see, Wolf," he explained. "The whole earth seemed like it was alive with shadows . . . squirming and moving. That was interesting, but then this other shadow . . ." He tried to describe it, without much success. "I am sorry, Wolf. It seems foolish now. But it was very real."

"No, no, it is good that you came to me," Wolf protested. "But tell me. How big did this shadow seem?"

"I could not tell. It changed, grew larger and smaller."

"Bigger than a man?"

"Oh, yes. A little bigger. As big as a horse, maybe. Sometimes not that big. Well, look, Wolf, at the lone willow, there, a bowshot away. It was near that, once. I thought the shadow was that of the tree for a moment."

"*Aiee*, that is maybe twice the height of a man!"

They looked at each other for a moment, each hesitant to say his thoughts.

"Hawk," asked Singing Wolf finally, "could it have been the real-bear?"

"I do not know, Wolf. That is why I came to you."

"It is good. But let us say nothing to the others. I do want to ask a tracker to look near your willow, there. I will ask Sees."

"He will laugh!" said Hawk in alarm.

"No. I have spoken to him of this before."

"You *have*! Of what?"

"Of the strange things this season. Bears that leave no tracks. He, too, feels it."

"*Aiee!* Sees wonders at this too?"

"Yes. He will understand. But he will say nothing either."

"It is good," said Hawk with obvious relief.

As it happened, the tracker found nothing of great significance. He tried not to be too obvious in his search. He even waited until after most of the People had left. Then he rode by a circuitous route around the column, to approach it from the left front. Sees reined in beside Singing Wolf, and rode casually for a little while.

"I found nothing," he said conversationally. "That means nothing, of course."

Wolf nodded, trying to appear casual.

"There were some tracks near that tree," said Sees. "They *could* have been made by a bear. But they were trampled. That was a busy place as the band moved out, you know. Does your father know of our questions?"

"No. Well, not recently. I talked with him after the lovers were attacked."

The tracker nodded. "There is one more thing, Wolf. My horse."

"What?"

"My horse. He knew something that I did not. I could hardly control him near Hawk's tree, there."

"Did he smell bear, maybe?"

"Maybe. But I am made to think he also sees things we do not. Things of the spirit."

Wolf nodded. "Some horses do that."

"Yes."

"But now we still do not know whether it is a spirit-bear or not," Wolf mused.

"That is true. Let us talk of it again." He started to rein away, but turned back. "What about Hawk?"

"I will tell him. He will say nothing, Sees. He was embarrassed to tell what he thought he saw."

"It is good," Sees said. "But he will keep watching, too. And talk with your father! Does anyone else know your doubts?"

"Only my wife, Rain. She helps with my medicine, you know."

"Of course. It is good."

The tracker rode away, mingling casually with the other travelers.

There was one more incident which seemed insignificant at the time, but Wolf recalled it many times later. He went one morning to bring the family's horses as the band prepared to break camp. The animals, some two or three hundred, were herded together each night by the young men who were about to achieve hunter and warrior status.

Wolf caught his own horse and swung to its back, beginning to sort out their two *travois* animals and Rain's mare to drive them back to the camp. He noticed another mare that seemed very excited, running back and forth through the herd, nickering loudly.

"What is the matter with her?" he asked one of the horse herders.

"She cannot find her foal," the youngster said.

"Where is it?"

"We do not know. She has been like that all night. But she stays with the herd, and does not go to look for it."

"Have you looked for it?"

"*Aiee*, Uncle, we have all these others to worry with. And they have been a little crazy too! She has them all excited."

The mare trotted past again, calling for her foal, her dripping udder swinging between her legs with the fullness of its unused milk.

"I hope she finds it soon," Wolf called to the herder.

The other waved in answer and rode on.

It was several mornings later that Wolf encountered the same young man again, and recalled the frantic mare.

"Did that mare find her lost colt?" he asked.

"What? Oh, no! That was strange. She is over there. It took her only a few days to get over the loss."

"You never found it at all?"

"No. Her owner, Fat Antelope, searched most of a morning, but found nothing. Maybe it wandered off."

With the hundreds of animals to look after, Wolf realized, the young men could not be concerned with one small foal. It was odd, though, that a mare would not remember where she had bedded it down the night it was lost.

Unless, of course, it was dead.

7

》》 》》 》》

During the Sun Dance there was very little thought of the real-bear, except as the stories were told. Amid the hundreds of people and lodges and dogs and horses, the possibility of a bear's presence was unthinkable.

In fact, to the others, the story of the bear problems of the Southern band was a minor part of the gathering. So an old woman who blundered into a bear's winter den had been killed last season? Such things happen. There were other events to discuss, visiting and games and preparation for the religious cere-monies of the season. It is likely that no one outside the Southern band really understood the dark threat that now hung over that group. For this occasion, they were trying to ignore it, but it was there. It was only pushed aside tem-porarily in the bustle and excitement of the fes-tival.

Behind the scenes, there was some discussion. Walks in the Sun sought out the camp of the Red Rocks band. There was an old friend there who might be of help and advice in the matter of the bear. This man was not even of the People, but had been born a Head Splitter, one of the nations who were friends and allies. His name in his own tongue, in fact, had been Bear's Head. When he had joined the Red Rocks band of the People, such a name was repugnant, and he was called Caddo Talker because of his ability to speak that language.

These two had become friends on an expedition to the south in earlier years, and now Walks in the Sun sought his advice. Head Splitters had no taboos about bears. They hunted them, and bear meat was considered a delicacy among their people. Surely, someone who had been named Bear's Head in his youth would be of help in this problem.

He entered the camp of the Red Rocks, and was directed to the lodge of Caddo Talker. His friend's wife greeted him at her doorway.

"*Aiee*, Walks in the Sun! My husband will be glad to see you, Uncle. He has gone to visit some of his relatives."

"There are Head Splitters here?"

"Yes. They usually come with our band. His people have no Sun Dance of their own, you know, so they attend ours. I think he is with them . . . See, the lodges at the bend of the stream?" She pointed.

"Ah, yes, of course. I will look for him. Your family is well?"

"Yes, fat and happy." White Flower smiled. "And yours?"

"All is well." He decided not to bring up the details of their current dilemma at this time.

"It is good. Tell Deer I will see her later!"

"Yes. We will visit later."

He turned and walked toward the cluster of Head Splitter lodges at the bend. It would be good to visit as families, but he needed the opportunity to consult with his friend first, alone. As it happened, Caddo Talker himself was sitting in front of one of the lodges, visiting with an older man.

"*Ah-koh*, my friend!" Caddo Talker called. "Here, join us. You know my kinsman, Long Sleep, I think?"

Walks in the Sun nodded.

"Good day to you, Uncle!"

He sat, and tried to conceal his impatience as they smoked the almost ritual pipe of friendship and made small talk about the weather and the game. But the amenities must be observed.

Finally, the pipe was empty, and Caddo Talker took his leave of his relative's lodge.

Walks in the Sun, too, paid his respects to their host, and the two left the lodge to return to the main encampment.

"It is good to see you again," Caddo Talker began, as they walked across the open space toward the larger camp. "You spoke to Flower?"

"Yes. She told me where to find you. Talker, I must ask your wisdom about something."

"*Aiee!* It is usually I who ask yours!"

Both chuckled. They were two of the few survivors of an ill-fated expedition to the south long ago. They had suffered much together, and knew much of each other's hearts.

"Not really," Walks in the Sun denied gently. "But this is a matter of which you must know much more than I. It is of bears."

"*Bears?* But you have a bear taboo, no?"

"Yes, Talker, that is part of the problem."

"How can this be, my friend?"

Walks in the Sun briefly recounted that portion of the Creation story that deals with Bear, and the agreement not to harm each other.

"Yes," said Caddo Talker, "that was my understanding of it. Then what is your problem?"

"Well, your people hunt and eat bears?"

"Yes, of course. I do not do so now, since I

live with your people. I could, I suppose, but there has been no need to do so. Why do you ask these things?"

Now Walks in the Sun poured out the whole story. The death of the old woman, the ensuing episodes, and the close encounter of the young lovers more recently.

"Now," he finished, "we are not certain whether this is an ordinary bear, or maybe a spirit-bear. Or, even, whether it really follows us as it seems to do. I have not been sure, but have had my doubts. We have talked, my son and I . . . you remember Singing Wolf? *Aiee*, Talker, he shows much promise as a holy man."

"What does he say?"

"Well, as I started to say, we have talked, but not much. Now, you know more of bears and their ways. Can you tell me?"

"Ah, I do not know . . . what are your questions? And this is a real-bear, the standing-up-walker? That makes it more dangerous!"

"Yes, we know. Now, first, what of spirit-bears?"

"Uncle, you would know more of that than I. You are the holy man. But any creature, I suppose, could be a spirit-being. My people, if they failed to kill it in the hunt, might think so. Of this one . . ." He shrugged.

Walks in the Sun nodded, not satisfied, but

understanding. "Then, if it is not a spirit, but only an ordinary real-bear, is it not acting strangely?"

"Yes, it would seem so. My people would hunt it until it was killed, and that would solve our problem. But you cannot do that?"

It was half question, half statement.

"That is true," the holy man admitted.

"Tell me, then," Caddo Talker went on, "would there ever be a time when your people could kill a bear, even to defend your lodge or family?"

"No. It would break the agreement."

Caddo Talker nodded sympathetically.

"Of course. What is the penalty for breaking your pact with Bear?"

Walks in the Sun took a deep breath and sighed. "We die," he said simply.

"*Aiee!* No exceptions?"

"None."

"What is the manner of dying, my friend?"

"That is not part of it. It could be an accident, sickness, anything."

"No connection to the bear, then?"

"It could be. Maybe, maybe not."

"Ah . . . I see your problem. If this bear continues . . ."

"Yes, that is it. You understand, Talker, I am not certain that we still have a problem. There has been nothing since we arrived here."

"Too many people," grunted Caddo Talker. "Even real-bears avoid this big a gathering. I feel that way myself, sometimes."

Both laughed.

"I, too," agreed the holy man, "but I have responsibilities."

"I know. But it is good to see you, old friend. We will talk again."

"Wait," said Walks in the Sun. "One more thing. Would you consider going with our band this season? If this bear is still with our Southern band, you could be of great help."

Caddo Talker was silent for a few moments, apparently lost in thought.

"I am made to think," he said finally, "that it is not good. What could I do?"

"Well, you have knowledge of the bear's ways."

"To hunt it, yes. But you do not hunt them. Wait . . . you want *me* to hunt it?"

"No, I . . ." Walks in the Sun was embarrassed. "It would seem so, though I was not thinking of it that way. You *could* kill it without breaking the taboo, I suppose."

Both were deadly serious now.

"My friend," said Caddo Talker finally, "you know that I would do almost anything for you. I owed you my life at several times long ago. But I am made to think that this cannot be. You know that it is not the danger that I fear. It is that I cannot interfere in your Covenant with Bear. That is between your people and Bear since Creation. It might even be that to ask me to do it would break your agreement."

"That is true. Forgive me, my friend. It was wrong for me to even think of it."

"No," insisted Caddo Talker. "You did not ask me to kill your bear. You only wondered about it."

Both laughed now. Their friendship was old enough and deep enough that nothing of this sort could have shaken it.

"So," Caddo Talker continued, "you have a problem, but it is between you and Bear, and I cannot help you."

"That is true," his friend agreed. "But we are not even sure of that. Maybe it is already over."

"Maybe," agreed Talker, "but I may join you this season anyway. It should be an interesting thing to watch. I will see what White Flower might think of this."

"It is good. Her thoughts on such things are good. It would be pleasant to have you join us."

"We will think on it, then. There is time . . . the Sun Dance has not even started yet."

8

»»»

In the end, Caddo Talker and White Flower elected not to join the Southern band for the season.

"We could be of no help," he told his friend. "It would only cause me a heavy heart if you found trouble, knowing that I could not help you. Besides, it is far from home. You can tell us of it next year at the Sun Dance."

The Southern band decided to travel into the heart of the tallgrass prairie, their Sacred Hills, for the summer season. The journey would not be long, probably half a moon. Preparations for departure were begun as soon as the last day of the Sun Dance was completed.

Even so, it was two or three days before the first of the big lodges began to come down. The Mountain and Red Rocks bands, who had the longest journey to their summer camps, were most anxious to begin. Farewells over, the long columns of horsemen, people on foot, *travois*, driven horse herds, and innumerable dogs began to wind their way across the prairie.

It was yet another day before the Northern band packed up and left their camp. But this year, there was one difference. The Eastern band, for reasons known only to themselves, had decided that they would not be the last to depart. It was a futile gesture, of course, to try to change their image. The other bands watched and laughed at the frantic attempt to organize and leave before the Northern band could do so.

The Southern band, with the shortest journey, was in no hurry at all. They did not have the social pressure to prove anything, and were rather enjoying the prospect of being the last to leave, at their leisure. It was a full day after the departure of the Northern and Eastern bands before they were ready to go. There were many jokes and much laughter over the Eastern band's hurried departure. Surely, the effort to live down their long-standing reputation had been less than useless.

The New band, trying hard to adjust to the ways of the People, were ready to go before the last of the Southern band's stragglers. They still traveled and camped near their sponsors, but were quite careful to create no inconvenience. They would travel in a close parallel, and would share the duties of the roving wolves to protect the flanks of the entire double column.

So it happened, contrary to the usual sequence of events, that the last stragglers out of the great Sun Dance encampment were those of the Southern band. Two families seemed disorganized. As those who were already packed began to poke fun at them they became even more inefficient. Finally one of those was ready. But the last lodge, a childless couple whose packing should have been simple, seemed unable to ready themselves.

"Was your grandmother not from the Eastern band?" someone called in derision.

Limping Elk, not known for his even temper anyway, yelled back in angry defiance. This alarmed his *travois* horse, which sidestepped over one of the poles, breaking it. A friend offered to help replace it, but Elk's temper was too far gone.

"Go on," he yelled. "I can do better without your help."

There comes a time when the joking and ridicule have gone too far. It was apparent that any more delay would further anger Limping Elk and add to his troubles.

"It is good," said the friend who had offered help. "We will see you later."

The head of the column had already formed up and was beginning to move. Those nearer the angry Elk and his wife discreetly withdrew and joined the general exodus.

The stragglers could catch up. There was little actual danger in remaining at the site of an abandoned camp of this size. No enemies, even had there been any, would waste their time in such an area. Likewise, a place that carried the heavy scent of man would be shunned for some time by all animals, both the hunter and the hunted.

In time, Limping Elk's anger at the entire situation would be a joke. For now, it was time to drop it and move on.

It was some time after midday that one of the scouts rode up beside Wolf's horse.

"*Ah-koh*, Hawk," Wolf greeted. "How is it with you?"

He was cheerful, enjoying the day and the sights and smells of the rolling hills. What is so fine as a sunny day in the Moon of Roses among the Tallgrass Hills? One can see, from many of the higher elevations, more than a day's travel in all directions. The sky is at its very bluest, and the world is good.

It was with some degree of surprise, then, that Wolf noted an expression of concern on the face of his friend. They had spoken little since the night when Hawk thought he saw the real-bear.

"What is it, my friend?" Wolf asked.

"I . . . maybe nothing, Wolf," Hawk said thoughtfully. "But I was riding behind this morning, one of the wolves in the rear."

"Yes, I saw that."

"Well, you know of how Limping Elk made a fool of himself and then stayed behind?"

Wolf chuckled. "Yes, so I heard."

"Well . . . I kept looking back. I have not seen them."

A chill of doubt flickered across Wolf's mind. But . . . it would take some time, would it not?

"*Aiee*, Hawk, they will probably not catch up until night camp."

"Yes, that is true, Wolf, but we should have *seen* them. Look, that ridge behind us. I stood there and searched our back trail. I could see even farther than the Sun Dance camp, but could not find them."

"They were in some low spot just then," suggested Wolf.

"No, Wolf. I have watched all morning. That was my duty today. There has been no time at all that I could see them."

Now Wolf became more concerned. It was no longer possible to deny the doubt that gnawed at him. This was something that must be investigated.

"Where is Sees?" he asked. "Let us tell no one else."

"I will find him."

"It is good. Let me tell my wife what we are doing."

Plans were quickly made. The three would quietly leave the column and meet on the back trail. Surely, thought Wolf, there could be nothing amiss. They would soon meet the stragglers, and ride with them to overtake the main column.

The tracker was not so sure. He seemed to expect the worst.

"I am made to think," he observed, "that it is the real-bear."

Wolf said nothing. Maybe he had merely been unwilling to voice his fears, he thought. Young Hawk, whose moonlight experience had perhaps been more impressive and ethereal than anyone's, still seemed quite concerned. After all, they were riding into an unknown situation. All three had at least some inkling that this was a possible tragedy.

They were almost back to the Sun Dance site before they saw any sign at all. Wolf was beginning to be concerned about their ability to overtake the main column before dark. It was mid-afternoon, and even with the long days of summer . . .

"*Aiee!*" exclaimed Sees. "Look!"

It was a horse, standing alone and unmoving. They turned aside to investigate. At the sound of their approach the animal threw up its head in terror and bolted away.

"That is Limping Elk's *travois* horse," said Hawk. "Look, it drags broken poles!"

The simple rawhide straps and ties that had held the poles in place were torn and pulled askew. One loop of hide around the animal's withers prevented the entire *travois* from falling free.

It was some time before they could get close to the frightened creature, but eventually they were able to persuade it to let them approach. Its hide was crusted with drying sweat, indicating a panicky flight. Most chilling, though, was the presence of four deep cuts, running parallel down the left hip, nearly to the hock.

"*Aiee,*" said Hawk softly. "The bear!"

With little conversation, they cut the dragging poles and straps, releasing the horse. It stood, still excited, shivering just a little as it stared around, wide-eyed.

The three remounted and hurried on. They reached the first of the circles where lodges had stood, and Sees pointed ahead.

"There!"

The woman crouched in terror, huddled against a tree, her eyes wide with fear. They were without focus, staring at nothing, and she babbled incoherently to herself. As they approached her, she screamed in terror and retreated, scuttling sideways on all fours like a crawfish.

"It is all right, Mother," Hawk coaxed her softly. "We will not harm you."

The tracker was moving quickly but deliberately among the debris of the abandoned camp, studying the ground. He came trotting back, his usually stoic expression showing much excitement. And maybe, thought Wolf, a little fear.

"What is it, Sees?" he asked.

"I am not sure. It is the bear . . . tracks at the stream. There is the blood of a kill."

"*Aiee!* Limping Elk?"

"I do not know. It could be a dog . . . But the woman . . . her husband missing . . . I am made to think that *he* was the kill. Wolf, we should leave now. It will soon be night."

They looked around nervously, their glances lingering for a moment on the more dense growth of trees and bushes along the stream. Any of a hundred places could conceal a bear. Wolf felt the hair rise on his neck.

"How do you know it is the same bear?"

"There are tracks. I know them from before. Come, we must go!"

Wolf had never known Sees to be so excited before. The tracker usually presented a calm and confident demeanor. This reaction was completely out of character for him. It was also contagious, and Wolf fought down a moment of panic.

"The woman . . ." He pointed.

The horses were becoming nervous, uneasy from the scent of blood, perhaps. But the scent of fear itself has an excitement about it, producing more fear.

Hawk was still hovering over the cowering woman, talking to soothe her. She was calmer now, but the blank staring look in her eyes was not good.

"Her spirit has gone," said the tracker, his voice tight.

It seemed true. The sheer terror of what she had seen had frightened her spirit so badly that it had fled from her body, leaving an empty shell.

"Will it return?" asked Hawk.

"Maybe," Wolf guessed, "maybe not. But we cannot leave her. We can catch that pack horse for her."

"Let us leave here," Sees urged. "The horses are getting more excited. They smell something." He swung to his horse and started to lead the way.

Wolf was amazed. Here was a man who had never been known to show cowardice, unashamedly afraid. It was quite unsettling to see.

Hawk now lifted the demented woman to his own horse and vaulted up behind her. They left the camp site behind, with little time to spare as the shadows grew long and Sun Boy splashed his paints across the western sky. Maybe it was only coincidence that tonight many of the splashes were as red as blood.

9

》》 》》 》》

It was a long ride that night, following the trail of the Southern band back to their evening camp. Every bush, tree, yes, every shadow seemed alive and threatening. They talked very little.

They had managed to catch the pack horse that had pulled the ruined *travois*. The woman rode it, while Hawk led the animal on a rope around its jaw. Even so, progress was slow. They could not move faster than a trot, and even that was hard to maintain. The senseless woman kept bouncing around and falling off when they trotted.

She also kept up a constant flow of gibberish, nonsense sounds that seemed like some other language. It was a horrible thing, riding along in the darkness, knowing the terror that lurked behind them somewhere in the night, and listening to the babbling of the mad woman. From time to time she would scream, a nerve-shattering shriek that brought chills to Singing Wolf's very marrow. It was always unexpected, just when things seemed calm and secure for a moment. The horse on which she rode would panic, and Hawk would fight to retain control. Then they would start on, and the insane babbling would begin again.

Wolf wondered if another spirit had taken the opportunity to enter the woman's body when her own fled in terror. It must have been a spirit in desperate need, to choose such a place of habitation. The entire night was most uncomfortable. He had always enjoyed the soft purple calm of the prairie night, but he would never feel quite the same about it again.

He thought of the Head Splitters, who refused when possible to fight at night. The spirit of a dying warrior leaving the body in darkness might lose its way, the Head Splitters said, and would be doomed to wander in darkness forever. Maybe, he thought, one of *those* lost spirits had taken over the body of this unfortunate woman. He listened closely to the droning babble . . . no, it did not sound like the tongue of the Head Splitters. It did not sound like anything, actually. An occasional word or part of one was recognizable, but it seemed only the insane raving of one who has gone mad.

They tried for a little while as they rode to reconstruct what must have happened at the deserted camp. Apparently the doomed couple had never even left the site. They must have been still loading the *travois* when the great bear struck. Probably it struck at the horse first, shattering the *travois* and strewing their belongings across the ground.

As nearly as anyone could recall, Elk had had one other horse with them. Any others they might own would be with the horse herd. Probably Elk's mount fled in panic when the *travois* horse was attacked, and then the bear had turned on the two terrified humans. This poor woman—they could not even remember her name—had undoubtedly witnessed the death of her husband as he was shaken and broken by the great bear. Then the bear had carried his body away in its jaws while she sat helplessly screaming. It was no wonder that her spirit had fled.

Singing Wolf was thinking of another thing, too. He was curious about the tracks, and asked again.

"It is the same bear, Wolf," Sees assured him. "I told you I recognized the tracks. This bear has a scar across the pad of its left forepaw." He made a slashing motion across his left palm with his right forefinger. "So."

"From a wound? What could cause that?" Wolf wondered.

"I do not know. A sharp flint, maybe. A lance or an arrow. Even a ball from a thunder-stick. Whatever, it did not sweeten his mood."

It was a grim joke, and no one even smiled.

"Sees," Singing Wolf observed, "this is a worldly thing, a wound that leaves a scar."

"Yes."

"But we have wondered if this is a spirit-bear."

Sees was silent a moment before he answered.

"That is your skill," he said finally. "Mine is tracking. This *is* the same bear."

Wolf nodded, still confused.

"There are many things that I do not know, my friend," he admitted. "We will talk of this with my father. But this I know: if it is a spirit, it could come and go, in any shape, and could take any shape it chose, with scars or without."

They had moved on, hurrying as best they could, frankly fearful of whatever terror lurked behind them. Little more communication took place, and Wolf spent much time in thought.

He reviewed all of the incidents involving the bear, trying to solve the questions that eddied through his mind. Could it be that this was merely a natural set of circumstances? He reconstructed the recent moons with that in mind, considering each sighting or confrontation.

The first killing, that of the old woman at the windfall . . . that was easily explained. She had violated the Covenant, even though unwittingly. The result was evident.

Suppose that this was a bear that had followed the buffalo herds into the area and chose to den up for the winter. Still nothing out of the ordinary. Then, after that encounter, it had again denned up nearby. It had been seen again by the New band.

At the point of awakening, then, this bear would have a different outlook on the world. It had been in close contact with humans on at least one occasion. It had learned that they are easy kills. Wolf's neck hairs began to bristle at the thought. If such kills appeared easy, why would the hunter go to the effort of following buffalo? There was game in abundance, easy for the taking, in the cone-shaped lodges of the People. And it was said that a cougar, having tasted human flesh, seeks it again. Might not a bear also?

He shuddered. Had the People become hunted flesh for the giant real-bear? It seemed likely. It had followed the Southern band and its horse herd instead of the migrating buffalo. Where it had once picked off straggling bison, the old or infirm or the very young, now it chose humans, who were also weak and easy. *And their horses!* He now remembered the mare who had lost her foal. And yes, now that he had connected this, had he not heard several men mention that their mares seemed less fertile this year? Maybe they *were* fertile, but their foals had become the prey of the bear.

This all seemed to fall into place as he turned it over in his mind. It would explain many things. It did not, however, make him feel much better about anything. It was a very creepy feeling to think that they had been watched as they traveled, in exactly the same way a wolf watches a helpless buffalo calf. The People, who had always been hunters, were now the hunted.

And even that made no sense. The bear should respect the Covenant. Even if the unfortunate old woman had unwittingly broken it, punishment had taken place. It *should be over.* Yet it was not. *Why?* Was there something here that he was overlooking? Were the People, at least the Southern band, being punished for something, some transgression that they had unwittingly done?

If so, then there was something of the spirit-world in the bear's strange behavior after all. Once again, Wolf came back to that question for which he saw no answer. Maybe his father could help him with the—

His horse shied unexpectedly, and there was a noise in a clump of sumac beside the trail. Panic gripped him for a moment as an animal rustled through the growth. It emerged from the other side, intent only on escape. And it was small, low to the ground. White stripes on its head identified the creature as a badger. A small relative of Bear, perhaps, but no great threat. Wolf relaxed a bit. But wait . . . was this a sign of some sort, a warning? He did not know, but realized that he was so tense that he was jumping at shadows. *Aiee!* To shy at a badger. He must control himself!

He and his father must cast the bones and talk of this. Several questions had come to mind.

Suppose, for instance, that *Bear* breaks the Covenant? Should that not neutralize the pact? He struggled with that point in his mind. Suppose that this individual bear, for instance, had broken the agreement, and continued to do so. Could it not be stopped, as the People would be stopped for such an infraction? One who killed a bear would die. Should not a bear die equally for the same infraction? It was certainly a thing to consider. He must ask his father . . . under what circumstances may a bear be killed?

They traveled on through the night. All

the way, Wolf had the feeling that they were watched. He knew that it was probably *not* true, but the knowledge did little to ease the feeling. He knew that even if the real-bear was *not* staring at the four travelers from that dark clump of willow ahead, there must have been times that it had been. How many times, he wondered, had the great bear watched *him* and evaluated the chances of a kill? It was enough to make his flesh crawl. Flesh that, he realized, the bear had considered for its food.

Aiee, Wolf, he told himself. *It is not good to think such things.*

He glanced over his shoulder at the back trail and hurried his horse along the way. But it was not easy, in the dark night, to ignore things that he knew to be true.

The mad woman screamed again and he jumped. She had not cried out for a while, and so he was not prepared for it. *Aiee,* it would be good to reach the camp.

Eventually, they did see the fires of the People's camp ahead in the darkness. He glanced at the sky. The Seven Hunters indicated, to his surprise, that they were not yet midway in their journey around the Real-Star. The People would still be awake. Probably they would be, anyway, awaiting the outcome of this mission of mercy. Certainly, Rain would be concerned until he was again in her arms.

He wondered if the scattered points of light ahead were being observed by the real-bear at this moment. That was likely, though it may have stayed behind somewhere to feast . . . He wished he could forget that part. But it was certain that there had been many nights when their fires were watched. Nearly every night, perhaps. It was an uncomfortable feeling.

A thought now occurred to him: all during their stay at the Sun Dance, they had felt secure in the strength of numbers. There had been no fear of the bear. But in light of what they now knew, the great beast must have been there all the time. It had waited, quietly stealing a foal occasionally, waiting for another chance at a human kill. But why the Southern band?

He tried to tell himself that that part, at least, was coincidence. The Southern band was merely the last to leave, and it had been their stragglers who had become prey to the bear.

In his heart he knew better. The waiting bear had watched each of the other bands depart. It could have followed any of them, but had not. It waited. Waited for the Southern band. He did not know why, but he somehow thought that whatever breach of the Covenant was involved, it concerned this band, and this band only.

Having decided that, he looked ahead, and began to accept a gruesome truth. A large hunter, like a cougar or a bear, or a pair of wolves with pups, must make a kill every few days. In plainest terms, the body of Limping Elk was fairly small compared to a buffalo. It would be only four or five days, maybe, before the bear must kill again. It would follow the plain trail left by the hundreds of lodge poles straight to the Southern band. There it would wait in hiding, travel *with them*, and wait . . .

The returning party found that an unusual thing had taken place as the band prepared to camp for the night. It had been noted that three young men were missing; Wolf, Sees, and Hawk. Speculation began, and rumors started to fly. They had been together, it was said, riding behind the column, and had fallen victim to the bear.

To dispel such wild fantasies, Rain told the actual facts. Her husband, with Hawk and the tracker, had retraced the trail of the People to see why Limping Elk and his wife had not overtaken the main party. That was all. They should arrive soon at the night camp.

That would probably have been the end of it, except that some children, gathering wood for the cooking fires, had heard some crashing in the brush along the stream. They had actually seen nothing. It may have been a deer or some smaller animal, but in the aftermath of rumor and speculation, it became a bear. The lengthening shadows of evening added to the story.

In a short while, this tale became one with the missing couple's whereabouts and the fate of those who had gone back to look for them. The more levelheaded of the People scorned the stories, but they could not allay the fears as darkness fell. And fear is contagious. Great fires blossomed, much larger than needed for cooking, in an attempt to drive the darkness back.

Around these fires, the stories, rumor, and speculation mushroomed. No one had talked much of real-bears during the Sun Dance, but now that the distraction was over, the suggestions poured forth. It was a supernatural creature, some said. How else could it be that it was here, ahead of them? Had not the children seen it along the creek? Well, *almost.* It was only one step beyond that for someone to suggest there was more than one bear.

The theory was growing rapidly. Now that the Covenant had been broken, someone proposed, maybe Bear would discard it and seek human prey.

It was probably fortunate that before the argument could split the band apart, the rescue party returned with their tragic tale and the woman who had gone mad from what she had seen. This distraction had the effect of focusing on the one bear. Had not Sees said it was the same? Speculation that all bears had gone mad was set aside for the present.

But it was still there.

10

》》》

"**N**o, Wolf," his father snapped irritably. "Even if Bear breaks the Covenant, it does not remove the taboo. No one can kill Bear without expecting the punishment."

"Then the Covenant works only one way," Wolf argued. "Bear can kill the People, but we cannot kill Bear?"

"No, that is not it. You ask too much understanding. If we kill Bear, we will be punished, no? We have broken the agreement. The punishment, death. In one way or another, maybe nothing to do with bears. That is our part of the pact."

"But—" Wolf began.

Walks in the Sun held up a hand.

"Wait . . . if Bear kills us, he too expects punishment, to fulfill his agreement. It, too, could come in any manner, I suppose. But the fulfillment must not be decided by *us*."

"So we can do nothing? Father, I am made to think that this bear is out there, watching. It will kill again."

"That is true, maybe."

"But we cannot defend ourselves?"

"Not without breaking our vow."

"And if we break the vow, we *die!*"

"Yes."

"Has it been done?"

"Oh, yes! I once heard of a holy man . . . in the Mountain band, I think it was . . . He was suffering from the illness that makes one wither away. He knew he was dying, and to hasten it, he shot a bear cub out of a tree. He even skinned it and wore the skin."

"Aiee!"

"Yes . . . the next day, his horse kicked him in the head and killed him."

"But Father . . . was that not because the smell alarmed the horse and made him kick?"

"Maybe. But it does not matter, does it? He broke the Covenant, and he died. It is not for you to choose how, or for me. It happens."

"Even though it appears *justified?*"

"Maybe. Is the good from killing the bear greater than the punishment? Maybe so. The Mountain band's holy man thought so. He was spared the lingering painful death from the disease that was eating him."

"Yes," said Wolf slowly.

"So," his father went on, "he was able to gain that by his act. It comes down to this: is the gain worth the punishment?"

Singing Wolf was to think of this conversation many times in later moons. For now, he had another question.

"Father, suppose one of the People was raised somewhere else . . . Stolen as a baby, maybe. When he is grown he does not *know* he is of the People. Maybe those where he lives kill bears, like the Head Splitters do. If *he* kills one, does he die?"

Walks in the Sun laughed.

"Aiee, Wolf, I have heard many argue this. Some say yes, he must, to fulfill the Covenant. Others say no, not unless he knows of it. One cannot be responsible for something he knows not, you see. There are still others who say that he must not only know, but must *believe* that it will happen or it will not."

"You mean, there is that possibility? That it is *not* true?"

"Anything is possible, Wolf."

"Has it ever happened, Father? That someone killed a bear and did *not* die?"

"I do not know, Wolf. Not in my lifetime. If it ever has, it would probably be in our legends, would it not? But it would not be something to boast of, so stupid a choice. And at the last moment, would you be *sure* you did not believe? Just a flicker of doubt, and you are *dead!*"

Somehow, this conversation was taking an unusual turn. Wolf had the idea that his father suspected what he was thinking. The last sentence or two of Walks in the Sun's talk seemed to imply that he was trying to dissuade Wolf from making any such experiment.

"What do *you* believe, Father?" he asked.

The older man smiled.

"I do not know. Maybe it is not for us to know. But our elders have told us that it is true, the story of the Covenant at Creation. We know of no times when it was *not* true for the People. It is much like the gift of a holy man, my son. As I have taught you, misuse of the power of such a gift will destroy him who misused it. The Bear Covenant is much the same, maybe. If we break it, we die. So does Bear, probably, if he breaks it."

"Then why does this one *not?*" demanded Wolf.

"It will," assured the holy man.

"But *when?* And why does the killing go on?"

Walks in the Sun spread his palms and shrugged.

"I do not know, Wolf. You have always asked too many questions. Some things are not meant to be understood. And how do you know, my son, that it is not *already* over?"

Wolf could not answer that, he had to admit. There had not been any signs of the bear for several days. Everyone was beginning to relax a little, but Wolf had his doubts. There was the matter of Fox Woman, the woman whom they had rescued and brought back. She was still completely out of her mind. When it came right down to it, no one actually knew what she had seen. Whatever it was, it was enough to destroy her entirely. She neither ate nor slept, and it seemed only a matter of time until she starved to death. Her relatives had all but started to mourn for her. It would be a relief when she was able to finally cross over. Maybe she had already done so, and was only an empty shell, no longer Fox Woman.

As he considered all these things, Wolf began to feel that somehow he was destined to have his own life closely intertwined with that of the bear. He had begun to feel it last fall, at the time of the bear's first kill. When others, even his gifted father, were willing to shrug it off as an unfortunate incident, Wolf had developed the odd feeling that the worst was yet to come. So far, he had been right, and the feeling was still growing stronger. He had been startled at his father's suggestion that maybe it was over. He knew better. Moreover, he thought that his father felt much the same, despite his reassurances.

They cast the bones separately, out of sight of each other. Wolf watched the little fetishes and bright stones and carved bones dance and skitter on the painted skin when he tossed them from the cup, marking their behavior carefully before they came to rest. Then the interpretation. He pondered a long time, and even made another cast to be sure. The result was the same. He sought out his father, who had been engaged in the same ceremony, as they had decided.

Walks in the Sun emerged from the lodge, and Wolf could see that his father was shaken. *His cast is the same as mine,* he thought. The older man quickly came to the point.

"You were right, Wolf. The bones show trouble and death, and very close to us."

"Yes. The Southern band."

"Closer to us than that, I fear," Walks in the Sun said, his voice tense. "Wolf, this is not good. And I failed to see it. But you were guided to it. You felt it from the first?"

"Yes, we talked of it. I did not know *what* I felt."

"Ah, but I was thinking only of the bear becoming a nuisance. Now I am made to think, my son, that this is a very mystical and spiritual thing."

"Then what must we do?"

"Only try to watch and listen. I am made to think that there may be nothing we can do."

"*Nothing,* Father?"

"Maybe not. But be ready to listen and act. Oh, yes, I spoke to our friend Caddo Talker at the Sun Dance. He is a Head Splitter, you know, and they hunt bears."

"Ah! Can he hunt this one for us?"

Even as he spoke, Singing Wolf knew the answer. This was a thing of the spirit, and there was also the taboo, carried out since Creation.

"No. This is between us and Bear, as it was in the beginning. We must handle it as best we can, because the problem is ours."

"Of course, Father. I realized that as I spoke. We only watch, listen to the guides, and wait then?"

"Yes, I am made to think so."

It was hard to foresee any danger, or any need for concern, in the pleasant surroundings of the summer camp. This was a favorite area for the People, one that was familiar to them. Plenty of grass, and a good river of crystal-clear water that tumbled over white gravel shoals to rest in deep pools in the stream bed.

The rest of the Moon of Roses gave way to the Moon of Thunder. Noisy storms marched across the prairie. Rain Maker beat his great drums in the sky, and orange flames flickered in the blue-black clouds. Occasionally Rain Maker tossed a spear of white real-fire toward the earth. Even so, it was not a bad season. None had been harmed by Rain Maker's spears. The rains had produced a good growing season for the grasses, and in turn the promise of a plentiful fall hunt.

Even Singing Wolf had nearly convinced himself that there had been a change in the situation of the bear. There had been no sign of the animal's presence—if animal it was—since they had arrived at the summer camp site.

When the sign did come, it was not intrusive, but quite insignificant. Singing Wolf would occasionally ride out alone, away from the confusion of the lodges, to meditate. He had found this to be a valuable way in which to make himself receptive to any guidance that might come his way.

Today, however, he was not even thinking of the bear. He had ridden in the bright sunshine across green hills, simply enjoying the beauty of the day. The sky was of purest blue, completely cloudless. That in itself was an omen for good. Aimlessly, he made his way up a small canyon toward its head. If this was the one he thought he remembered, there would be a small but clear spring at the head of it. Maybe he should stop a little while and let his horse drink and graze. Ah, yes, there it was!

He swung down and approached the rocky pool on foot, leading his horse. It was not until he had dropped to his knees to drink that he saw the track. The rim of the little pool was rocky. There was only one place, where the water spilled out to trickle downward, that there was a small flat area of mud. A couple of yellow butterflies sat there, sucking moisture from the damp soil, and he was looking at them when he saw the outline. A footprint, not quite human, much longer than his own, with huge claws at the tips of the toes.

For a moment he stared in disbelief, before he realized something else that sent a shiver across his sun-warmed body. Across the widest part of the footprint was a diagonal scar.

11

》》》

Wolf glanced quickly around, trying to fight the panic that gnawed at his gut. Even as he did so, he wondered why his horse had not reacted to the smell that must linger here. Was it the light breeze, moving *away* from the animal?

Whatever the cause, it was no time to ponder. He must leave the area, and quickly. He sensed again the odd feeling that he was being watched. It was a very uncomfortable feeling, like an actual physical pressure between his shoulder blades. Cautiously, he looked around the rocky little glen. There were dozens of places that could hide a bear.

There was a nervous snort from his mare, and he turned to look at her. Apparently there had been a change in the shifting breeze. The creature was now wide-eyed, nostrils flared, dancing as she rolled her head from side to side,

searching for a glimpse of the source of the terrifying scent that now assailed her nostrils.
Wolf knew that she might easily become unmanageable, crazy with fear. At the same time
he realized that if the mare pulled away in
panic, he could not hold her. He would be left
here with the dreaded bear, on foot, and prevented from defending himself by the taboo.

The risk was real and present. This was no
time for calm philosophic discussion. No
longer could he ask himself the theoretical
questions about "what if . . . ?" It was a matter of life and death, and there was no time.

Even as these thoughts flickered through
his mind he was starting to swing to the mare's
back. But she was fighting now, crazed by the
more clearly identified scent that spoke to her
primitive memory of terror and death. Wolf
spoke to her, trying to calm her, but the mare
was beyond that point. She turned and lunged
away, jerking at the rein. The rawhide burned
through his palm, and he frantically tightened
his grip against the pain. The knot at the very
end of the thong was all that stopped him from
losing the mare entirely. He fastened on that
knot with a death grip, fighting to hold her
. . . fighting for his life.

In pulling away from her would-be rider,
the frantic animal was now backing blindly
amid the uneven scatter of rocks and brush.

She tripped, her hind feet struck a low boulder, and she fell to her haunches.

Singing Wolf had never considered himself much of a horseman. Another man might have done it differently. Another, of course, might not have lost control of his mount in the first place. But now, Wolf saw the mare, helpless for the briefest of moments, and realized that for the space of a heartbeat he had an advantage that would soon be lost. The mare's broad back was before him. He took one long step to a low boulder and jumped from there, landing astride the horse. He heard the animal grunt from the impact, and hammered his heels into her flanks to get her to her feet. Many things could go wrong. She might try to roll over to get up. It might be, even, that the animal had broken a leg when she fell. He dared not think such thoughts, but had no time to do so anyway.

Like the jump of a cat, or the strike of a snake, the mare sprang out of her sitting position, and into a run. The leap was so sudden that Wolf was almost unseated, but he clung to handfuls of the horse's mane and bent low over her withers. Another long leap and she was on better footing. He glanced behind, but could not really get a look around the area. Merely staying in the saddle required his complete attention. The mare was scrambling, pushing back down the almost invisible game trail that she had ascended a little while ago. Brush clawed at his leggings, and once a glancing blow struck his knee as the frantic mare pounded past a rock at a bend in the trail. Wolf let her run. He could not control her anyway. As long as they were moving away from the spring where bear smell hung heavy in the air, it was good.

The mare finally began to slow, blowing hard. Gently, he pulled her down to a walk and turned to look behind him. He half-expected to see the towering figure of a giant real-bear standing on the crest of the rimrock, roaring in frustration at the loss of its prey. But there was nothing. Everything seemed quite calm. A yellow-breasted lark sang from its perch on a stone. A bright-winged grasshopper rose from the ground and clattered in noisy flight for the space of a few paces before it landed, invisible again as it folded its dull wing-covers. Pungent scents rose from sun-warmed prairie herbs. It was no more than a warm pleasant afternoon in summer, and no less. Had it actually happened? More accurately, *what* had happened? Anything at all?

What had he actually seen or heard, Wolf asked himself. It all came down to a single track in the mud at the spring. And, he now wondered, had he actually seen even that? Or had he only seen it so many times in his mind's eye that it now crowded into the real world?

No, it *was* real, he assured himself. There was no other way to account for the behavior of the horse. She had stopped now, and was standing, head down, still breathing heavily. Her hair was soaked with sweat, and as she stood, exhausted from her effort, she still trembled. Her instincts must have been valid. Wolf swung down to relieve the exhausted animal of her burden. She may have saved his life today.

He wondered how fast a real-bear can run. As fast as a horse? He did not know. He had never thought of that before, but today it had become quite important.

Yet another thought occurred to him while he waited for the mare to recover. She had reacted violently to the threat, probably to the scent of the bear. But not until after *he* had seen the track at the spring. The breeze had been wrong. It had been a very narrow escape, maybe. The more he thought of it, the more he became convinced. Somehow, he had seen the track and had taken warning. A few heartbeats later . . . Had the bear been stalking him, and stayed its charge because it was not quite ready for the attack? He shuddered, certain that he had been saved by coincidence.

But in a larger sense, *are* there coincidences? It occurred to him that maybe he had not been as attentive as he should be. He had been thinking of the cool fresh water of the spring, how it would taste and feel on his tongue. He had really not been alert, as he should have been. Fortunately, he had been forced to attention, even before the reaction of the horse. Forced by . . . what? He remembered words of his father, when Wolf had returned from his vision quest.

"I am made to think, my son," the holy man had said, "that yours is a powerful spirit-guide. You must listen to what your guide tells you. Listen, look, and feel always. Do not force the guide to seek you out. Be open, ready, and it will all be easier for you."

There had been many times when Wolf had felt the guide's direction. Usually he only realized it after the event. The solution to a problem that had faced him would suddenly become quite plain, and he would know that he had experienced spiritual help. He had discussed it with his father.

"I could not have done that alone, Father."

Walks in the Sun nodded.

"It is good. If you accept with thanks, it becomes easier." He smiled. "Does it not *feel* good?" he asked confidentially.

Now, standing beside his sweating horse, Wolf realized once more that he had benefited from the assistance of a higher power, that of the spirit. He had not been attentive, but in the moment of crisis his guide had found a way to catch his attention. The muddy track . . . Had it really been there? It had saved him, so it did not matter. Except that he must be grateful.

Wolf lifted his head and gazed deep into the clear blue of the sky above him.

Thank you, Grandfather, he silently prayed to his guide. And it was good.

It was some time before he judged that the mare was ready to travel. He did not want to push her too quickly, or he would further harm her, and he would be on foot, in a dangerous situation. Finally the labored breathing slowed, and the animal began to walk around, stiffly at first. When she started to nibble at the grass, Wolf laughed aloud.

"It is good," he told her. "You are ready now!"

He swung up and turned toward the camp. He was thinking as he rode about what he should tell of the afternoon's adventure. At first, it seemed a great event, but in thinking of it, was there really anything to tell? He had seen a bear track, his mare had become frightened, and he had come home. That would all seem quite commonplace to the listener. Maybe it would be best to downplay his experience. He would talk of it to Rain, of course. Maybe to his father, who would understand the matter of the spirit-guide. He would talk to Sees and Hawk, because that was important. They must know about the track, because the three of them were the ones who had realized from the first the great risk, the importance of this bear's threat to the People.

Yes, that was the importance of this day, he decided. He would tell his story, but only that he had seen the track, which showed that the bear was in the area. That would warn the People to be careful. Some were becoming overconfident, so this should help.

He could go into a little more detail with Sees and Hawk. He could talk of his guide's help with his father. And he could share the experience with his wife, who would understand his feelings.

There was one part of it that he could share with no one. He did not understand it, but he knew that it was becoming stronger. Somehow, there was a gripping significance in the fact that the bear was out there in the gathering shadows of early evening. Was it disappointed at having missed its prey? He was sure that his escape had been very narrow.

Wolf was becoming more and more convinced of a thing that seemed very odd to him. In some way, he and this real-bear, whether animal or spirit or both, were caught up in a strange series of events. He and the bear were connected somehow, and could not escape that fact. It made no sense, yet he was certain that as events unfolded he would learn more. Already he felt that over and beyond any tradition, any covenant or any taboos, his relationship to *this* bear would be a major event for the People. It would not be over until one or both were dead. He could not have said how he knew this, but he was sure.

This, of course, was something he could share with no one. Not even Rain, with whom he shared everything. And that part made his heart very heavy.

12

»» »» »»

The People listened to Wolf's warning, but there was no real excitement. There was a general feeling that with the death of Limping Elk it was over. So Singing Wolf had seen a bear track? That was not an unusual event.

After a few futile efforts, Wolf realized that to continue to cry his warning would be to lose his credibility. The People were not taking seriously the news of a single bear track far from the camp. Why should they? There was no way that Wolf could tell them of its importance and be convincing. He did not know, himself, how he knew, or why.

So life went on in the summer camp of the People. In their day-to-day existence problems not current were easily forgotten. Why worry until the problem arises?

It was frustrating to Wolf. Only a moon

ago, when the rescue party had returned to the
night camp to tell of Limping Elk's death, the
People of the Southern band had been dis-
traught with fear and rumor. He remembered
the wild speculation, how some had insisted
that Bear had overthrown the Covenant and
was beginning to hunt and kill humans.

In all truth, that possibility must be considered. With the strange happenings of the
past year, anything was possible. Wolf felt
fairly certain that all the incidents were related, but that the unlikely behavior was
linked to only one bear. But who could be sure?
Rain had told him of the near-panic on the part
of a few the night they had lost Limping Elk.
He had rejected the theory, but was now ready
for another look. He talked to his wife again.

"Rain, that evening, the day we left the
Sun Dance camp and Sees and I went back . . .
you said some children saw a bear?"

"No, they heard noises in the willows.
They thought it was a bear."

"Ah! No one looked for tracks?"

"No, I think not, Wolf. It was nearly dark,
you know."

"So no one really saw anything?"

"That is true, I guess. What are you thinking, Wolf?"

"Nothing. I was only wondering. You said

that some were saying that Bear—*all* bears—
had gone mad and were hunting people."

"Yes, that was said. It started an argument,
but just then you and the others returned. I
have heard no such talk lately."

"That is true. Until I found the track yesterday, we have heard little of bears."

It was strange how, with no present threat
of danger, such ideas were quickly forgotten.
The People had slipped easily into the comfortable summer routine. It was not yet time for
the great fall hunt, and there was no real urgency to daily life at this time. They would
stay in the lodges on days when summer
storms swept across the prairie. When Sun Boy
relit his torch they merged, and rolled up the
skin covers to let the breeze cool their lodges.

Singing Wolf felt an urgency, though. He
talked with his father of the theory of many
bears.

"I do not know, Wolf," admitted Walks in
the Sun. "I believed that there was nothing
more than that first kill, the old woman, you
know. We have cast the bones, which seem to
indicate bears, but how many? *Aiee*, it is a
strange thing. You said that the track you
found is the same bear?"

"Yes, I am made to think so. Sees told me
of the track of this one. A scar across the pad of
the left paw, here." He pointed to his palm. "I

recognized it from his telling of it. I have never seen this bear, of course."

"Nor have I. But let us think . . . Is there *anything* to indicate more than one bear?"

"I can think of nothing, Father. But how could we tell?"

"*Aiee,* I do not know. Tell me, has anyone seen other bears . . . at a distance, even? If all bears have gone mad, we should see that they are behaving differently, no?"

"True. Even black bears, not just real-bears?"

"Ah! I see what you are saying, Wolf. If Bear breaks the Covenant, then all bears . . . yes, it would be less dangerous to watch black bears. Someone could ride out and look . . . watch some."

It seemed a logical plan, and Wolf was pleased. This approach should at least answer the one question, whether *all* bears were involved in these strange events. He must talk to the others. He rose to go.

"Wolf," his father called, "did the woman ever talk to you of what she had seen?"

"Fox Woman? No, she has made no sense at all. I am told she is near death, Father. I will go and see her once more."

The widowed Fox Woman lay in her sister's lodge, blank eyes staring upward at the smoke hole. Dry yellow skin stretched tight over her cheekbones. Her babble was little more than a whisper now.

"Her spirit is gone," the sister said sadly. "She eats nothing. I give her water . . . a little soup. She cannot last much longer. I do not know how she has lasted this long."

"My heart is heavy for you . . . and for her," Wolf said. "Did she ever speak of what happened?"

"No. I am made to think that it left with her spirit. She does not know."

"Does she sleep?" he asked.

"Sometimes, a little. Then she cries out, and wakens. Or becomes like this again. Maybe her spirit tries to return and is frightened again."

"Maybe. Does she cry out about anything? Any one thing?"

"Oh, yes! Bears."

"One bear, or *bears?*"

"Ah, I do not know, holy man. Who knows? You have heard her."

Yes, he thought, *we heard her for a half day's journey*. Aloud he said, "Of course. My prayers are with you."

He rose and left the lodge.

Wolf intended to talk with Hawk and Sees the next day. It had been late when he finished his visit to the lodge of Fox Woman's sister. He had gone home, eaten, and was relaxing in the twilight, watching the children at play, when the wailing cadence of the Song of Mourning wafted across the camp. Wolf knew that it was finally over for the mad woman. She had crossed over. He hoped that it was a good crossing. He looked across the fire at Rain.

"Fox Woman," he said.

"Yes," his wife answered. "Will it be right for her?"

"I hope so. Rain, I must go and talk to Hawk."

He rose and made his way to the lodge of the young man's parents, where Hawk lived because he had not yet found a wife.

Somehow the passing of Fox Woman had added to the urgency of the whole situation. Wolf felt that he must do something. There had been at least three deaths, besides some narrow escapes. His own experience had been very disconcerting, and he felt fortunate to have survived it.

In addition, the loss of a foal or two every few days would prove a hardship to the People over a period of time. Though their affluence revolved around the buffalo, the means of securing that wealth lay in the use of the horse. So, fewer horses, less wealth. It was secondary, of course, but a hidden threat if the marauding of the bear continued.

Wolf tapped on the lodge cover and called out.

"*Ah-koh,* my friends. It is Singing Wolf. I would talk to Hawk."

Hawk emerged from the doorway and straightened.

"What is it, Wolf?"

"I would talk. Come, let us walk."

The two strolled toward the edge of the camp, where the lodges were spaced farther apart.

"You heard the Song for Fox Woman?" Wolf began.

"Yes . . . may it go well for her!"

"*Aiee,* I hope so! But this has nothing to do with that, Hawk. Yes, maybe it does. You have heard the thought that there may be more than one bear following us?"

Hawk nodded.

"Yes, some were nearly crazy with that on the night we found the woman."

"And then they seemed to forget. Ah, how quickly things change when things are going well."

"That is true, Wolf. When you found the track, no one paid much attention, did they?"

Wolf nodded ruefully. "Except for you and Sees. And my father, of course. I have talked to him."

"Is there something new?"

"Not really. We spoke of whether there is one bear or many."

"And what does your father think, Wolf?"

"He does not know. His medicine, like mine, tells of Bear but does not tell how many. But Hawk, would it not be a help to learn all we can of this?"

"Of course. But how can this be done?"

Quickly, Wolf sketched for his friend the basic theory: if the happenings of the past season indicated a change in the Covenant between the People and Bear, then the actions of all bears would be affected. If there was not such a change, it would suggest that only this one real-bear was involved. For whatever reason, natural or of the spirit, only one bear.

"Ah, yes," agreed Hawk. "Then we would know better how to avoid it. But Wolf, how do we learn this?"

"We watch other bears. Black bears. They are less dangerous."

"True. But if the Covenant is to be destroyed, they too . . . yes!"

Hawk became excited over the prospect of being able to do something about the problem that they shared.

"I will go out in the morning, Wolf. It should be possible to watch black bears. *Aiee*, how strange, to seek bears!"

He laughed to himself.

"Let us tell no one, Hawk," Wolf suggested. "I will speak with Sees, of course. He may have other thoughts. But I am made to think that we must learn all we can before the bear kills again."

"That is true. I will ride out tomorrow to see if I can find bears to watch."

A tiny hint of doubt whispered in Wolf's head. Was Hawk too confident?

"You must be very careful, Hawk," he cautioned.

The other laughed.

"Of course, Wolf. Have I not always been careful? I will have a fast horse and will watch only from a distance."

"It is good. We will talk again later. And I will speak with Sees in the morning. He will help us, too."

13

>> >> >>

Hawk lay on the ledge of limestone outcropping at the rim of the canyon. He had spent most of the morning riding along the grassy ridge, pausing to study each of the fingerlike box canyons for any sign of bears. Something had made him stop here. It was nothing he had seen, more like a feeling that *if I were a bear, here is where I would be.*

It was a wider cleft than some, with less vegetation. Fewer trees and brush, that is. The grass appeared thick and lush with the leafy growth of early summer. A canyon of this size would produce enough grass to burn well when the fires swept the prairie in the spring. This improved the grazing by destroying weeds and brush and encouraging the growth of the prairie grasses. A smaller canyon or gully would not make enough grass in most years to support the fire, so it would be choked with brush and small trees.

This particular canyon, Hawk noted, was grassy, an excellent place for grazing animals as well as for rabbits and other small creatures. In addition, there were scattered blocks of stone strewn across the canyon floor. Big, square chunks of white limestone like the one on which he lay. Those below, he realized, must have formed this rim many lifetimes ago. In the upper end of the gully was a jumbled pile of rocks, with many dark openings formed by their positions. That was what had originally caught his eye. There were probably small caves and pockets that would be quite suitable for dens.

Now add to that opportunity the presence of good grass . . . *yes,* he thought, *it would be good hunting, too, for bears.* He had tied his horse some distance back from the rim, to a heavy sumac stem. He left enough slack so his gelding could graze. It was a dependable horse, and would not become overly impatient while time passed. Hawk glanced at the sun, estimating when he must leave to reach the camp before dark.

He was not completely sure what he was looking for. There were many unknowns in the problem that faced the People. He had talked at length with Singing Wolf, and understood at least the general idea of what they were questioning. Both Hawk and the young holy man believed that the entire series of events revolved around one bear, the scar-footed real-bear. Well, Sees, the tracker, thought the same, did he not?

But there were those among the People who questioned that interpretation. Granted, they admitted, all of the attacks seemed to relate to one bear. However, if one bear had broken the Covenant, might it not be that it was *because all bears* had decided to reject it? Most of the People were not much concerned with the theological problems of the Bear Covenant, but there were always the few who would argue anything. Singing Wolf felt that they must *know* about this question in order to refute the arguments of these potential troublemakers.

Hawk was proud to be included among the elite who were trying to solve this mystery. It was a great responsibility, and he devoutly hoped to show his devotion to the well-being of the People. It was by chance, maybe, that he had been the one on watch on that moonlit night when the earth seemed alive with mystery. Or maybe *not* by chance. Maybe he had been chosen for this special service to the People.

Either way, it made him feel a great sense of accomplishment to be asked for his observa-

tions and opinion by such respected men as
Singing Wolf and Sees. Both were older than he,
and had already earned a certain degree of pres-
tige. Both were considered skilled, each in the
area to which he had been called. Hawk was
not yet certain what direction his own life
might take, but this was a chance to show his
dedication to a task.

This was why he now lay on his stomach,
watching the canyon below. The sun was hot
on his back, and he had become stiff from so
long in one position. Just now, he dared not
move. He had caught a glimpse of motion
among the jumbled blocks of stone at the canyon's head. Or maybe, he now thought, he had
only believed that he saw it. Maybe it was like
the shadow that flits past the edge of one's vision, and when he turns, it is gone. Maybe . . .
Well, he could stay perfectly still a little longer.

The rocky jumble was several bow shots
away. He had not wished to be any closer. It
would be too easy to alarm his quarry. If, of
course, there was anything actually living in
those crevices. It might be that he was only
wasting the day, that there was nothing there.
At least, nothing larger than a fox or a coyote.
Well, such a watch would be good anyway, a
chance to hone his skills of observation. He
could—

Wait! Yes, there again! A definite motion

in one of the crevices in the pile of jumbled blocks. Without moving, he fastened his gaze on that area. Now that he had that particular spot isolated, he could see, or maybe only imagine, that there seemed to be a faint trail, a path through the new growth of this year's grass. Yes, he was sure now. That crevice was in use. But by what?

He stared, unwavering, until his vision began to blur and he had to at least move that much, blinking to relieve the tension on his eyeballs. He did so, with some improvement. But now there was a tickling sensation on his left ankle. He dared not move to look. It might be a fly, or an ant, or any one of a number of small creatures. Or even a stray blade of grass. Even a wayward puff of air, stroking his skin . . . He reassured himself that whatever was creating the sensation, it was not likely to be anything significant or dangerous. This reassurance was not totally successful.

But now the motion below was repeated, and he forgot everything else. Yes! A dark form moved into the open, a slender head and dark furry body, moving gracefully over the rocks. Then a smaller one, and another. *Aiee*, a female and her two cubs, of last winter's birth. He smiled to himself at the antics of the cubs, playfully charging at each other, rolling and biting and cuffing in mock ferocity. One cub was somewhat lighter in color than the other, a dark glossy brown. The other was black, like the mother. This was not unusual among black bears.

This is good, he thought. A good place from which to watch, and a family of black bears. This female would not be aggressive or dangerous, unless someone threatened her cubs. Now what sort of behavior would he be looking for in this bear family? Hawk glanced at the sun again. Ah, a little more time . . .

The bear was moving along the slope where the wall of the canyon met the floor. She would pause to dig or to turn over a rock, and even from that distance, Hawk could see the cubs pushing with each other to be the first to grab whatever grubs or other small creatures might be exposed. They were amusing to watch, like small children playing in friendly competition at some game.

One of the cubs became too enthusiastic with the pushing and nipping, and the other squealed in pain. Instantly the female cuffed it soundly. *Aiee,* Hawk thought. *How much like a mother of the People!* It is no wonder, then, that the People had agreed to a Covenant with Bear at the time of Creation. Bear people are much like human people, after all.

Hawk could see no unusual behavior, but then, who knows what *usual* behavior is for a bear? At any rate, he reflected, he would be able, at least partly, to answer some of Singing Wolf's questions. There were other bears in the area, behaving as one expects a bear to behave. Black bears, surely no threat to the People. Hawk would be proud to report this to Wolf. He would watch a little longer, and then go. There was still plenty of time to reach the camp before evening. A little longer . . .

The lighter of the two cubs made a ferocious charge at the other, bowling it over in a tumble of black and brown fur. Hawk almost chuckled aloud at such human-like behavior as the cubs rolled and wrestled on the grass.

His thoughts were interrupted by a cry from his horse. It was a long, plaintive whinny, almost a thing of urgency. Then he heard the drumming of hoofbeats, becoming more distant even as he listened. He rolled away from the edge and rose to hurry toward the sumac thicket. He was more annoyed than alarmed. The horse had broken loose, and now he would have to chase it down. Well, there was plenty of time before nightfall. At worst, he would have to walk all the way to camp. If he did, the gelding would probably be there before him. It was logical for it to try to rejoin the herd.

Irritated at the thought, he pushed through the sumac growth, noting that it was a healthy-looking clump. The shiny leaves would be good to cure for smoking, mixed with tobacco. The flower heads were pushing their way upward at the tip of each plant. He would remember this place when the time came for the ripening of the berries, and the tart drink that could be made by boiling them.

These, of course, were instinctive, minor thoughts that came to him as he pushed through the thicket. His main thought was for the horse. Had that not been a cry with a touch of worry in it? Maybe even *fear?* Could the animal possibly have gotten a whiff of bear scent from the canyon below?

He became more anxious as he pushed ahead, and emerged into the little clearing where he had left the gelding. The sumac stem to which he had tied the horse was gone, completely uprooted. *Aiee*, the animal must have been crazy with fear, to fight the tether in such a way. And to run away, dragging what amounted to a small tree at the end of the picket rope!

Quickly he made a circuit of the clearing, looking for any sign that might be found. He wished that Sees were here, or that he possessed the tracker's skills. Some things he could tell. Here the grass was cropped closely. There, a pile of droppings. The animal had been standing undisturbed, and the moist surface of the lumps told him that it had been only a short while ago.

Then the torn sod and scattered soil that told of panic . . . hoofprints with the still damp margin blurred and more soil torn up and scattered when the animal whirled to plunge away in terror. A cold realization came over him, and he rose from his kneeling position over the hoofprints. Even as he did so he heard a guttural sound that sent a wave of terror through him. He whirled to look.

The giant form that towered over him, only a step away, seemed to shut out half the sky. He could see the rage in the shiny little eyes, and the real-bear opened its mouth to roar at him. The great curved teeth were longer than the knife at his waist, and he could smell its fetid breath, the head was so close above him.

Hawk stood rooted to the spot, unable to move as the great arm swung. He caught only a glimpse of shiny dark claws, knife-sharp at the tips, before they struck.

14

»» »» »»

"**W**olf, I would speak to you!" the man called from outside the lodge.

Singing Wolf lifted the flap of the doorway and stepped out. It was the father of his friend Hawk, and there was a look of concern on his face.

"Have you seen my son?"

"No. Is he missing?" Wolf asked.

It was a question, he thought, that must have seemed quite stupid. If Hawk was not missing, his father would hardly be searching for him.

"He has been gone all day, and has not returned," the worried parent responded. "I know that he talked to you last evening. Can you help me?"

"Ah, I wish I could, Uncle. Hawk was going out to scout, but I do not know where. Did you ask the horse herders?"

"Yes. He has not returned his horse to them."

Wolf looked around the camp. It was nearly twilight. The shadows lay long across the earth, and the colors of the sky lent a strange glow to the objects within view. Lodges, trees and bushes, even people moving around in their evening chores were bathed in otherworldly color. To Wolf it seemed ominous. He was certain that Hawk would not be out alone after dark. Hawk knew too much.

Wolf was uncertain whether Hawk had shared their concerns about the real-bear with his parents. And if so, how much? It would be unwise to say very much about it now, until he learned more of what Hawk's father knew.

"I will see what I can find out, Uncle," Wolf promised.

He paused only long enough to tell Rain where he was going. She nodded. She had heard much of the conversation from inside the lodge.

"Be careful, Wolf," she said seriously, her eyes wide with concern.

"Of course. Am I not always careful?"

He embraced her for a moment and left the lodge, wishing that he was really as confident as he pretended. He spoke again to the concerned father of Hawk.

"I will see what I can learn, Uncle," he promised. "I will come to your lodge later."

The older man nodded, and they parted.

Wolf wanted to consult with the tracker, but first he wished to talk to the young men who had been with the horses. They might know something that would be useful. It was possible, even, that Hawk had mentioned which direction he intended to ride. Of course, it was likely that those who watched the herd now had not been there when Hawk had saddled to ride earlier in the day. However, maybe they could help him find whatever herder had last seen him.

Dusk was deepening as he approached the herd. It was usual to quietly move the animals into an area somewhat nearer the camp as night fell. Wolf approached a youth who was seated on an old mare, watching the grazing animals spread across the meadow before him. The youngster was probably pretending that he was a noble warrior or a great hunter. At least, that was what Wolf had done when he had fulfilled this duty.

"*Ah-koh!*" he greeted.

"*Ah-koh*, Uncle." The young man smiled, his teeth white in the gathering darkness.

Wolf was not yet accustomed to this traditional term applied to himself. "Uncle" was the proper greeting among the People for any

adult male older than one's self. Still, it seemed
odd to be addressed in this way. Wolf thought
of it as applying to his father or some of the old
men of the band. For Sees, even, though the
tracker was only slightly older than himself.
But such is the way of things.

"Yes," he answered uncomfortably, returning his thoughts to his unpleasant task.
"Can you tell me who might have been herding
earlier today? This morning, maybe, when our
brother Hawk left to scout."

"Of course, Uncle. Someone said he had
not returned. Is there trouble?"

Wolf tried to keep his voice calm and level.

"Maybe not. But I wanted to talk to him.
He has not returned, then?"

The young man spread his palms in helplessness.

"*Aiee*, Uncle, I do not know! I have not
seen him. But the herd is large. He could have
come in at the far side."

"Yes, that is true," agreed Wolf. "Now,
about who might have been here this morning . . . ?"

"Ah, yes. Three Dogs, maybe. Broken
Oak—"

He was interrupted by a call from one of
the other herders, who now trotted up and
pulled his horse to a stop.

"Ah, Uncle! I did not know you were here. It is good. You know our brother Hawk?"

"Of course! What—?"

"His horse . . . anyway, I think it is his. A bay gelding?"

"Maybe. Tell me! *What?*"

"Well, a horse just wandered in dragging a picket rope, and wearing a saddle."

Wolf's heart sank, but he tried to maintain his composure.

"I wish to see the horse," he said. "Can you show me?"

"Of course, Uncle."

Wolf turned to the other young man, the one to whom he had been talking.

"You know the lodge of the tracker, Sees?"

"Yes, Uncle. You want me to bring him?"

"Yes, but quietly. Let us tell no one of this until we know more."

"It is good," the youth agreed as he reined away.

"Come with me, Uncle. I will show you the horse," the other young rider said. "This way!"

Wolf walked beside the horse, partway around the circumference of the meadow where the herd rested. Some of the horses grazed, some lay at ease. But they were quiet. That, at least, was a good sign.

"There!" announced the young man,

pointing. "Is that not the horse of Hawk? I did not try to remove the saddle."

"Yes, it is Hawk's horse. Let us look more closely."

Wolf was trying to estimate whether there would be a moon tonight to furnish a little light. It was a little past the full moon, so it would rise somewhat later. Meanwhile, they could tell little in the deepening dusk. But he must try.

The horse was skittish as he walked toward it, hand extended. He talked softly, and after a couple of false attempts, managed to grasp the dangling rope. Once he had managed that, the horse quieted under the influence of control. Wolf touched its nose and ears, breathed into its nostrils, and crooned softly to it.

"It is all right now, my brother. You will not be harmed."

The horse calmed quickly now, and he could begin to make a few observations, even in the poor light. The trailing rope was tied to a stick, somewhat thicker than his thumb and as long as his arm. *So it must have been tied*, he thought, *and broke away*. He felt the neck and shoulder, crusty with dried sweat. He thrust his fingers beneath the saddle . . . Damp, but cool. At least as cool as the gelding's normal body heat.

Gently, he ran his hands over the animal's body, feeling the legs all the way down to the fetlocks. He could find no injury.

The other herder now returned, accompanied by Sees.

"What is it?" asked the tracker. "Hawk's horse, they tell me?"

"Yes," Wolf answered, "and it does not look good."

Sees quickly examined the gelding, much as Wolf had done, talking softly to himself. Finally he straightened.

"*Aiee*, Wolf, you are right. It is not good! I am made to think it was this way: the horse was tied, and broke loose. We do not know how big this tree might have been where it was tied. It may be a sumac stem. We can tell with better light. But it has been broken, the horse has stepped on it, dragged it. He was badly frightened when he broke loose."

"*Aiee*, how do you know that, Uncle?" asked one of the young herders.

"Well, look . . . It is a thick stem, where he was tied. He pulled away and then ran, ran hard. There is heavy dried sweat on his hair. And it was shortly after midday, but before late afternoon."

Wolf was pleased that he had estimated nearly the same. The sweat was dried, and the animal cool, so it had been some time since the panicky flight took place. While Sees explained this to the young men, Wolf's thoughts were racing ahead.

It was obvious that Hawk had not been riding the horse, or it would not have been tied. He may have been nearby, but when the frightened gelding pulled loose he had been unable to catch it. The animal had then run until it was exhausted, and then wandered back to rejoin the herd.

And what of Hawk? That question became larger and more alarming now. Unless he had been injured, Hawk should have been able to walk back almost as fast as an ambling horse. The horse would stop to graze and look around from time to time. Realistically, Hawk should have been able not only to overtake the horse after it quieted, but to catch it. Yet he had not. Had Hawk been injured somehow, or was the horse so terrified that it would not allow the rider to overtake it?

The tracker was finishing his explanation to the herders. Wolf was pleased that Sees did not go into detail in his speculation about the rider.

"Let us unsaddle and take the rope off," Sees was saying. "He probably has a sore mouth from dragging the rope."

It was quickly done, and Sees picked up the saddle.

"We will take this to his parents' lodge," he told the young men. "Then tomorrow as soon as it is light, Singing Wolf and I will go and search for Hawk. Now, let us say nothing of this until we know something, no?"

Wolf agreed with this approach, but feared that it was unlikely that Hawk's disappearance could be kept quiet. After all, his father had been inquiring about him.

The two walked back toward the camp, saying nothing at first. It was Sees who broke the silence.

"You saw it much as I did, no?"

"Yes. I am made to think this is not good."

"That is true. If Hawk is alive, he is unable to walk. And I would not want to be out there in the night with whatever scared the horse this badly."

"I, too, Sees."

"I will meet you here at daylight?"

"It is good."

Though, of course, the situation was not good, neither of them wanted to voice that which hung heavy on their thoughts. It was highly unlikely that Hawk would be found alive, if he was found at all.

15

>> >> >>

The tracker circled and crisscrossed in the direction from which the gelding had returned until he picked up the animal's tracks. Singing Wolf rode slightly behind him as they headed out, to avoid destroying the trail they sought.

It was not long before Sees pointed ahead. "It came from that ridge over there," he stated. "There is a canyon beyond with several finger canyons off it. I have been there before."

They moved a little faster now, with Sees sometimes pointing out the tracks for his companion. Occasionally they crossed a few tracks of the outgoing trail, but the tracker's attention was focused on the meandering tracks of the loose horse on its return.

"Ah!" he said suddenly. "Hawk's horse spent some time here, probably after his run. See, he stood here and fidgeted around, ate a little grass there, and then started to wander back home."

They were on the treeless, gently rolling flat top of the ridge. They could see the camp in the distance by the smoke of its fires, and it was plain that anyone on this vantage point could watch the comings and goings below. *Anyone or anything*, thought Wolf. There was an ominous feel to the morning, and both were well aware that whatever they might find, it would not likely be good.

As Sees had already surmised, the back tracks now indicated that the loose horse had been running frantically until it stopped, exhausted. It did not take long to trace the trail to a thick clump of sumac.

"It was tied there," Sees observed. "We must be careful now."

It was a worrisome thing to approach a spot where they knew that something had happened. Something terrifying enough to send an experienced buffalo horse running in a panic to escape. Cold sweat coated Wolf's skin, and he could feel his heartbeat.

"Let us circle this thicket," suggested the tracker. "Whatever scared the horse is probably gone now, but maybe we can find tracks."

Cautiously, they rode around the thicket, trying to peer into its concealment. They were about halfway around when their horses began to react excitedly. Both Wolf's mare and the spotted horse of the tracker were tossing their heads, rolling eyes in alarm, and snorting nervously.

Sees swung down. "Here, take my horse and go back around a little way," he suggested, handing the rein to Wolf. "There is something I want to see."

"Be careful, Sees," cautioned Wolf. But the tracker was already kneeling over something. The horses were becoming calmer as they left the place where they smelled whatever was alarming them.

"Something was dragged here," Sees called. "A kill . . . The horses smell blood."

Wolf's heart sank, though this was what he had feared. Now the tracker was pushing into the sumac. Wolf started to call out for caution again, but realized that Sees was in a better position to judge the danger than he. And Wolf now realized that the tracker was following the *back* trail into the thicket.

It was not long until he came back into view, visibly shaken. In one hand he carried a moccasin, and in the other a broken bow. Wolf recognized both as those of Hawk.

Sees hurried back toward where Wolf held the two horses. They became excited again, and the tracker stopped, glancing at the objects in his hands. He held them up, allowing them to tell their own story, and then tossed them aside. They carried the scent that would continue to drive the horses into crazed irrationality. The scent of blood, death, and bears. Wolf had been able to see, before the tracker tossed the objects away, that both were blood-smeared. It was plain what Bear's kill had been.

Sees swung quickly to his horse, and without a word led the way at a trot, back toward the camp. They were a couple of bowshots away from the thicket before he spoke. His voice was tight and unnatural.

"The horse was tied in there," he said. "I am made to think that Hawk was watching the canyon over there, and the horse became frightened and pulled loose. When Hawk came to see about it, the bear was waiting."

"The same real-bear?" asked Wolf, though he knew the answer.

"Yes. One track in the blood shows the scar. *Aiee*, Wolf, it is as if this bear leaves his mark for us so there will be no mistake!"

"Then there is no chance Hawk is alive?"

Sees looked at him strangely. "None," he said. "Wolf, I have never seen a bloodier kill. The bear almost tore him apart right there. There are scraps of his shirt, scraps of . . ."

The tracker paused, seemingly unwilling to finish the sentence. "Wolf, we must get out of here."

"Could you tell where the bear went?" asked Wolf.

"That way . . . along the rim. Toward the rocks, there. It is too dangerous to follow."

He kicked his horse and broke into a lope. Wolf could see that the tracker was completely demoralized by the episode. And *afraid*. Again he marveled at the change in the man. An odd thought struck him. Do trackers see things not given to others? He did not know, but realized that each has his own gifts. Maybe the gifts that had been given to Sees were letting him see too much.

The camp was alive with rumor and dread when they rode in. It was apparent from their faces that their message was a sad one, and the Mourning Song was beginning even before Wolf reached the lodge of Hawk's parents.

"It is as we feared?" asked Hawk's father.

"Yes, Uncle," Wolf answered. "I am sorry. He was a brave man."

A scream came from inside the lodge, and Hawk's mother burst out, crying in her grief, throwing handfuls of ashes over her head. Wolf sat uncomfortably on his horse, unsure what to do or say.

Hawk's father spoke again, a simple question. "His body? Can we . . . ?"

Wolf shook his head. He was unable to

speak, so powerful was the emotion that he felt. He tried to swallow the lump in his throat.

"The bear?" asked the stricken parent, more steadily than could be expected.

Wolf nodded. "I am sorry, Uncle. There is nothing else we can do . . . except to mourn."

He reined away.

"Thank you, Wolf!" the bereaved father called after him.

That was perhaps the hardest of all.

There was a council that evening. It was time that the crisis was discussed publicly. Past time, maybe. There were angry accusations about lack of leadership, and venerable old Broken Lance, still the band chief, finally showed the diplomacy that had made him a leader for many winters.

"My brothers," he said calmly, "it is no time for anger, here. We have a matter to deal with. It has been a hard one, a puzzling one. In my lifetime, I have never heard of such a thing. But some of our best have been working on it. Walks in the Sun and Wolf, the holy men, Sees, our finest tracker, and young Hawk, who has given his life . . ."

The old man paused for dramatic effect, and Wolf was once more impressed. He had no idea that the old chief was aware that they had been so involved in the matter of the bear. Here was truly a leader. Wolf felt embarrassed, almost, that they had not done more to inform him. But of course, there had been little to tell.

Now Broken Lance was speaking again.

"Some have wondered," he observed, "if all bears have gone mad. I would hear from our brother, Walks in the Sun. What say you, holy man?"

"I am made to think not," Walks in the Sun observed. "But most of the thought in this matter has been done by my son, Singing Wolf, and the others you have mentioned. I would defer to them, my chief."

Broken Lance turned to Wolf, who was somewhat embarrassed to speak unexpectedly before the council. He rose and cleared his throat.

"My chief, I have studied this at great length, with the help of Sees, here, and our departed brother. I would point out that no one of the People has seen much of this creature. We have been made to know of it by its kills."

There was a mutter in the crowd, and Broken Lance raised a hand for quiet. Wolf proceeded.

"I do not know whether this is simply a bear gone mad or a spirit-bear. Are we being told something we do not understand? But I am made to think that whatever its nature, this is only one animal, the same each time, and not all bears."

"And why do you think so?" asked the old chief.

Wolf had an idea that Broken Lance already knew, but wanted it explained to the crowd.

"I can do no better than ask our brother Sees, the tracker, to tell you," Wolf offered.

Sees rose, embarrassed also at the attention, but understanding the importance of his testimony.

"You realize," he began, "that neither Wolf nor I have ever seen this bear. Those who have say that it is a real-bear, a very big real-bear. This would be true, from the tracks I have seen. Each time there has been a kill, I have found the same track. Yes, it is the same bear, *one* bear, and I stake my reputation on it."

The tracker sat down, and there was silence for a moment. No one wanted to challenge the reputation of this respected man.

The chief spoke quietly.

"Do either of you, or you, Walks in the Sun, have any suggestions, anything we should do?"

Wolf and his father exchanged glances. It was plain that they had none. Then, to everyone's surprise, the tracker spoke again.

"I have," he stated. "This bear has tasted

human flesh, and found that it is easy to catch. It will continue to kill. I do not know its spirit, but I know its ways. I am made to think we should move the camp. Quickly, in the morning. Maybe we can leave it behind."

Now there was a murmur of discussion, and some mild argument. But it was a strong recommendation.

A leader will be forgiven for almost anything but inactivity. In an emergency, leaders make mistakes. Their followers will forgive this, but they will not forgive a leader who does nothing. A good leader knows this by instinct, and recognizes the point at which he must do *something*, even if it is wrong, hoping to be forgiven because he tried.

Broken Lance was a good leader. He knew that there is a time to do nothing, and that time was past. Now he must act.

"It is good!" he announced. "Tomorrow, we move!"

He clapped his hands to indicate that the council was over, and the People scattered to begin the chores of packing for the move.

It is good, thought Wolf. *Much better to do something, instead of sitting and waiting.*

In the excitement of the activity of the coming day, he had not yet stopped to realize that they had moved before, and the bear was still with them.

16

>> >> >>

The sun had hardly cleared the horizon before the first of the lodges came down. Many of the People had been up all night making preparations.

The plan was to move westward for a few days, halting when it seemed right. There was little concern as to how they would know that. It was a thing to decide when the time came, and that obviously was not yet.

Singing Wolf had his doubts as to the effectiveness of this plan. There seemed no reason to believe that the bear would not follow them again, as it had for many moons. However, he understood that it must be tried. The People were restless, and it would help to have something to do. He came close to understanding the cunning leadership that had always been effective for Broken Lance: be quietly visible when things are going well. When they are not, announce a decision. Almost any decision, within reason, will provide the distraction that is needed.

Wolf also talked with his father again and cast the bones to try to foretell the success of the move. The results were equivocal, at best.

"Sometimes it works well, sometimes not," Walks in the Sun observed. "We will see."

To Wolf, it seemed that the forecast might be overclouded by the coming of the fall hunt. This was perhaps the most important event of the year, after the ceremonial Sun Dance festival. The hunt would be carried out by each individual band, and on its success or failure rested their winter food supply. Usually it was successful, because the great migration of the herds took place at this time. Since the coming of the horse many generations ago, the hunting of the buffalo had been much easier. The old legends of the Moon of Starvation when food became scarce were hardly more than that . . . legends. It was called the Moon of Hunger now, and even so, it was not an urgent problem. At least, not in years of normal weather patterns.

Wolf was pleased to see that his casting of the bones foretold a highly successful fall hunt. In a way, this might help their ongoing problem. If the hunt did prove quite successful, there would be large quantities of food for the scavengers. Vultures, coyotes, the larger gray wolves, and even the great bears that followed the herds.

He began to wonder if it might be possible to move again, to leave the area after the hunt, but while the four-legged hunters were still occupied with the leavings. He finally realized that it would not be very practical. It would take several days to dry, process, and pack all of the fresh meat. The People were limited by the time required to do this. Bear had no such limitation. He would eat that day's meat immediately.

Another possibility occurred to him. The first bear kill, nearly a year ago, had been when the old woman had blundered into the bear's winter den. Might it be possible to delay the People's move to winter camp until after the bears had settled for winter sleep? That would leave their problem behind. Wolf could see some dangers in such a plan. The weather in late fall could be quite unpredictable. It could be a real threat if Cold Maker swept across the plains with an early storm while they were still traveling. Time was required to set up winter camp. More time than the casual summer moves. It was hard to realize this in the heat of the Red Moon, the hottest part of the summer. Still, Wolf felt that the idea of a late move to leave Bear behind might hold some merit. He set it aside for now.

The column moved out as usual for travel. There were no stragglers today. Although nothing had been said or done to ensure it, the column was as close and efficient as it had ever been. The New band, smaller and trying hard to adapt their ways to those of their new allies, elected to move with the Southern band. It was good. They had many skilled hunters who would help in the fall hunt.

Yet another idea kept recurring to Wolf as he rode. Might there not still be some way in which these allies might hunt down the dangerous and troublesome bear? He knew that his father had consulted with a Head Splitter friend about such an arrangement. Even so, it might be worth another try.

Then an odd thought occurred to him. The New band had not suffered from the depredations of the real-bear. They had *seen* the animal, seen its tracks, but not one of them had been killed, or seemingly even endangered. Why? Was the whole series of events aimed at only the *Southern* band? If so, why would it be so?

Maybe, he thought, Bear still resents the intrusion into his winter sleep. Maybe the old woman's People are still the object of Bear's vengeance. Surely, though, that has now been repaid. Maybe this time it really *is* over. Or if not now, *when?* What would indicate that the vengeance was completed, and that the Covenant was once more in effect?

Wolf thought of going to his father with this line of reasoning, but was reluctant. He believed that he knew what his father would say: *Wolf, you want to understand too much!* Well, he would think on it, anyway. There must be some way to know when an end point is reached and it is really over.

They traveled for six days, moving fairly rapidly. They had moved out of the tallgrass hills and into a flatter country, where the vegetation was of different types. Cottonwoods and willows were still common along the streams, and there were some sycamores. But the giant oaks and walnuts were no longer in evidence. It was the shortgrass country, where vast areas seemed to produce nothing but curly blue-green buffalo grass. The People knew its value for grazing. Sweet to the taste and rich in nutrition, it was dependable for the buffalo, as desirable in its way as the taller and heavier grasses of the Sacred Hills.

The Southern band seldom came this far west, preferring the rolling hills and the lush grasses that were taller than a man in the autumn. But drastic times demand drastic measures. The buffalo would migrate through the shortgrass region too, and as Wolf had noted, the signs promised a good fall hunt.

The question was whether this move had succeeded in its main purpose, avoidance of further problems with the real-bear. Wolf found it almost amusing sometimes that most tribes or nations that the People knew could have solved this problem quite easily. They would simply hunt and kill the individual bear that was doing the damage. But of course, other nations had no pact with Bear that dated from Creation.

Broken Lance decided on the site for their late summer camp. It was well chosen, Wolf thought. Good grass, available water, and good visibility. It was possible to see for a long distance, and that was good. Not only could the approaching herds be seen to signal the fall hunt, but a creature as large as a real-bear would be visible for quite a distance. This shrewd choice of sites was not lost on Singing Wolf.

In a half-day the camp took on the appearance of home. The familiar lodges rose like so many giant mushrooms, in the same relative positions as before. Door openings always faced east, so anyone looking out his own doorway saw essentially the same scene as he had in the last encampment. The same lodges with patterns or family designs, those of friends and relatives in the same positions as always.

The eastern direction of the door openings had a multiple purpose. One was symbolic, to welcome the rays of Sun Boy's torch each morning. From a more practical standpoint, however, this was the only efficient position. The movable smoke flaps above the doorway must be adjusted to open quartering downwind, in order to draw the smoke properly. In the prairie, the prevailing winds are from the south, so adjustment is easy. In unsettled weather, winds may come from north, northwest, or southwest, but rarely from the east. Thus, practicality and centuries of practice have determined customs which then become symbolic and religious. Above all, the people of the prairie are practical.

For the same reason, the scouts circled the newly established camp for some distance out, acting as wolves, familiarizing themselves with every bit of the terrain, every rock, bush, and gully. It was surprising, how in a country so flat, a slight rise or fall of the terrain could conceal objects.

The New band camped directly across the stream. "Stream" was an exaggeration, perhaps. In the Red Moon of summer, streams in the flatland are largely sandy washes. But there is water beneath. Legends of the People say that such streams flow upside down.

By dark, people were digging in the sand, enlarging holes that still held some water, or creating new seep wells for drinking, cooking, and for the horses. For the Southern band, accustomed to the clear cool springs of the Sacred Hills, this was not the most desirable area. Still, it was inhabitable. If it would help in the removal of the curse of the bear, it was well worthwhile. This shortgrass country was not really bad, they told themselves. It should be a good area for the fall hunt. And any slight rain would probably raise the water to fill the banks of the stream bed to overflowing. This led to caution in placement of the lodges. No one wished to lose his lodge to a flash flood.

By nightfall the camp was settled. There was a spirit of optimism. Surely the unusual move, the fast travel in an unexpected direction, the departure from the normal summer routine, had been successful. There had been no sign of the dreaded real-bear during the journey. The People had high hopes that the crisis was over.

Singing Wolf helped Rain set up the lodge and build the symbolic first fire. This would announce their presence to the spirits of the place, and ask their good will.

Sees rode up, dismounted, and waited a

moment while Wolf offered a pinch of tobacco in the fire, a gift to the spirits. His face was long, and as Wolf turned to look at his friend, his heart sank. He knew without asking, but had to do so.

"You have seen . . . what?"

The tracker shook his head.

"We have failed, Wolf. He is here."

"The bear?"

"Of course. We should have known we could not escape."

"What have you seen?"

"Only a few tracks. That is all. But one of them is the one with the scar."

Wolf was not surprised. It was as if the creature wanted them to know. An identifying mark, like the designs on the lodges or on the shields of the warriors. An announcement, almost:

I am here. You cannot run away.

The two decided to withhold the information for the present. They would tell Walks in the Sun, and he could relay the information to the chief if he thought it advisable. But there seemed no point in creating panic on the first night in a new camp. Spread the word tomorrow to be careful, without being too specific.

Wolf did share the find with Rain. There was really no choice. Sees departed, leading his horse, and Rain came out of the lodge at about the same time. She stood looking at her husband for a moment, then came and placed an arm about his waist.

"He is here, isn't he? The bear?"

Wolf looked at her blankly and nodded.

"Aiee," she whispered. "When will this end, Wolf? *How* will it end?"

He shook his head.

"I do not know."

17

》》》》

Despite the grim warning, there was no sign of the bear. The People settled quickly into the new routine. There was despair at first when they learned that the bear's tracks had been seen. They soon recovered their confidence, though, and with each passing day paid less attention to the danger. There were even jokes about the tracker, and doubts that he had seen anything at all.

"Sees is becoming an old woman," one youth joked. "He probably saw his own footprint!"

It was true that Sees had been deeply affected by the events of this season. He would have been the first to admit that his courage had suffered. Where once he had boldly pushed ahead, he was now cautious, almost fearful. The tracker's son was so concerned that he came to talk to Singing Wolf. Crow was a shy young man, of perhaps fifteen winters, never a spectacular achiever, but thoughtful, like his father.

"Uncle, I would speak with you," he began, "about my father."

"Of course. What is it?"

Wolf knew the youth only by recognition, and did not feel that he knew him well enough to understand what was wanted.

"Well . . . he has changed. He does not sleep well. He worries."

"*Aiee!* I see. I, too, have worried."

"You mean, about the bear?"

"Yes, maybe. We have thought much about this, your father and I."

"I know, Uncle. That is why I came to you. My mother is worried, also. We think my father has lost his courage."

"Does your mother know you came to me?"

"No. I only thought to ask you. Sees has never feared *anything*. But now he seems to be without courage. I would not speak ill of him, Uncle, but only wish to find help for this."

"I understand. And yes, he is my friend, and I have never known a braver man. You are right to be proud of him, Crow."

He saw the gratitude in the young man's eyes, and hurried on.

"Now, about the bear . . ."

"Yes?"

"This is a thing of great importance . . . of concern, to your father and me. It is a danger to the People."

"Yes, so he says."

"So do you not think this is much of his worry?"

"Yes . . . do you worry, too, Uncle?"

Wolf smiled, a wry smile.

"It would be stupid not to worry, no? But I am made to think, Crow, that he worries not just for himself but for the People, as I do."

"You think he does not have fear?"

"Of course he has. Crow, a man who says he does not have fear is not only a fool but probably a liar, too. Your father is no fool. He knows when to have fear. I think he worries, as I do, that the People do *not* have much fear right now."

"I see. They need to think of this more seriously?"

"Yes, I am made to think so. Your father thinks the same, maybe. We will help each other all we can, so that we can better help the People."

The young man smiled.

"It is good, Uncle. Now I must go."

He started away, and turned back, a look of concern on his face.

"Uncle, you will not speak to my father of this talk, that I came to you?"

"No, no. I will say nothing."

Crow nodded and hurried away. Wolf watched him go, aware of the troubles that disturbed the sleep of his friend the tracker. Sometimes the People seemed so unseeing. When some incident grasped their attention they could think of nothing else. Then, if nothing further occurred, their attention wandered to other things. It was certainly like that with this trouble of the bear. People alternated between extreme concern and a careless nonchalance that was almost a denial.

"Maybe it is over . . ."

What irritated him most strongly was probably the fact that he found the same attitude in himself. It was easy to fall into the trap, because of the basic tendency of the People to meet one trouble at a time, as they occurred. And this, Wolf was certain, was a trouble of a different sort. It was an ongoing thing, for which he could see no end, except some climactic event that would provide assurance of relief from the dread that now followed them.

Even so, it was difficult not to appreciate the long golden days of late summer. It was hard to believe that they could hold any evil.

It was even harder when an expected distraction came. One of the wolves loped into the camp and pulled his horse to a sliding stop amid the lodges. This raised a cloud of fine sandy dust, as well as the ire of the women in the area. The irritation was quickly forgotten, however, in the importance of his message.

"Buffalo! The herds come!"

The People hurried out for a glimpse of the distant herds, flowing from the north like a dark stain over the lighter colors of the prairie. It would be another day or two before they came close enough for the hunt. Maybe longer. But they were here, and the excitement of the fall hunt was in the air. The next days, the next moon, would be occupied with hard work on the part of everyone. But it would be good, because of the results. A good hunt would ensure a comfortable winter, with little hunger and no starvation.

For the immediate future, as the work progressed, there would be the joy of abundant fresh meat, of the delicacies of fresh liver and other choice cuts, cooked even while the work progressed. It was a time of joy in accomplishment, the culmination of the cycle that had begun with the return of the Sun, the grass, and the spring migration. Now the season would be complete, the promise of the Sun Dance fulfilled.

Plans for the hunt began immediately, directed by the leading men of the warrior societies. A leader of the hunt was elected that night at a council called for the purpose. The wolves would watch the herds as they approached, reporting the direction of flow to the leader. Then the strategy would be planned.

Meanwhile, there would be absolutely no hunting. To go out on one's own would possibly disturb the natural progress of the migration, and could destroy the effectiveness of the entire hunt.

Under these circumstances, the threat of the bear's presence was completely forgotten by nearly everyone. Even Wolf was distracted, though not entirely. It was a time of optimism, and he was by nature an optimist. Maybe, he thought, in the presence of plenty, the bear would find it easy to scavenge the leavings of the season's butchering. Bear, like the vultures and coyotes, would be satisfied, and would have no need to hunt. He tried to convince himself of this, and to choke down the doubts that nagged in the deepest corners of his mind. The fall hunt, with its completion of the cycle, had always provided the satisfactory end of the season. It was easy to see this as the end of a troubled time. This would surely be depicted in the paintings on the Story Skins of the People as the Year of the Bear.

But it was nearly over. In the days between the sighting of the herds and the start of the

hunt, Singing Wolf managed to convince himself that this was true. For the People as a
whole, the hunt was bigger than the threat of
the bear. Later, he would wonder how he could
have been so wrong.

The hunt was good, the planning flawless.
A segment of the herd was carefully separated
by slow-moving horsemen, and maneuvered
into an area where the footing for horses would
be good for the chase.

And *aiee*, what a chase! Singing Wolf, who
had sometimes used the thunderstick, left the
weapon in its case now. Reloading on horse-
back was too cumbersome and slow. Besides,
the use of the bow brought back the excitement of his youth. There was a thrill like none
other in charging up alongside a running buffalo to drive an arrow into its ribs. His horse,
too, was caught up in the excitement, even biting at the flank of one intended quarry as they
drew near its right side.

Buffalo were falling, and it was already apparent that the kill would be good. Wolf
thought that he had accounted for three, possibly four. He was unsure of the fat young cow
that had turned at the last moment, just as a
running bull had jostled his horse. But no matter. His arrows would identify his kills when

the butchering began. That was another advantage over the gun, he reflected.

This year, however, with meat in plenty, there should be no question as to whose meat it was. There was easily enough for all, more than could be dried and stored. That, too, was good, thought Wolf as he began to come down from the thrill of excitement. There would be not only meat in plenty, but leavings in plenty for the meat eaters who would begin to gather.

As the butchering parties began to organize and flow onto the scene of the hunt, Wolf saw a pair of coyotes standing on a distant rise, watching, waiting. High above, a circling black speck floated nearer, like the weightless black ash when the prairie burns in the spring. Another, circling . . . The vultures, too, were gathering.

He rode back to his first kill, dismounted, and addressed the head of the young bull with the ritual apology.

"We are sorry to kill you, my brother, but upon your flesh our lives depend, as the grass feeds yours. May your people prosper and be many forever."

He went to look for Rain and the children. Other women and children were scattering among the carcasses and beginning to strip the skins.

By afternoon a great deal had been accomplished. Great quantities of meat and many skins had begun to be processed. There were still some kills to be attended, and a few had built fires for light near the carcasses where they still worked.

It was at one of these fires that the incident occurred. Three women were working together. They had finished stripping the carcass of a young cow at a distant margin of the hunt area and had moved to a closer kill to accomplish a little more before night. It was not fully dark yet, and they were discussing whether to build a fire.

"Aiee!" exclaimed Dog Woman. "I left my skinning knife at the other kill! You start the fire, and I will be right back."

The fire was not even blazing yet when they heard the scream. It seemed to be cut short, and there was a chilling silence, except for the sound of coyotes quarreling over a more distant kill.

18

»» »» »»

Consternation struck the Southern band.
Their attention had been diverted from the
problem of the bear. Some, who had not been
in close contact with any of the previous kill-
ings, had begun to scoff. It is always easy to
advise another when it is not your own lodge
that is threatened.

But the success of the fall hunt, the total
absorption with the necessary work, the joy of
plentiful supplies for the winter . . . It is
doubtful that many had even thought of the
danger that day. And then, as it had happened
before, when least expected, one of their number had been struck down.

Word passed quickly through the camp.
Dog Woman had gone back to where they had
been butchering to retrieve her knife, just at
dark. They had heard her scream. It was

quickly apparent from the choked-off sound of the scream that it was useless to try to help her. There was, of course, some effort to mount a rescue party. But this was a special situation. It was assumed that the tragedy involved the real-bear, so what good would come of an incursion into the deepening dark of the night? If they encountered the bear, what could be done? The warriors could not attack it, because of their Covenant with Bear. This particular animal had already shown disregard for the Covenant, so it would surely attack them.

Now, would it not be foolish to knowingly walk into a situation such as this, forbidden to defend one's self, yet certain to be attacked? Men who would have gone into a battle that was virtually hopeless now backed away from this. The known danger combined with the mystical threat of the supernatural was a situation to be avoided.

The family of Dog Woman, unable to do anything else, began their ritual of mourning. It was apparent that she could not be alive. Other families abandoned their tasks and the meat of their kills and hurried to the comparative safety of the camp. Fires were piled high to drive back the darkness, and no one slept. The primary goal tonight was survival. Tomorrow would serve to salvage what meat they could.

Maybe they would have to mount another hunt. If it came to that, so be it.

Singing Wolf sought out Sees. The tracker was in his lodge, blankly staring at nothing. In the flickering light of the fire, the tracker's face looked pale and drawn. He looked up, his expression unchanging, listless.

"It is as I said, Wolf."

"Yes. What can be done?"

"Nothing."

"Some of the men talked of going out with torches."

"What could they do?"

"Yes, I know," agreed Wolf. "They have given up the idea. No one wants to go."

"I will go in the morning," Sees offered.

"Not now. We can look, but . . ." His voice trailed off.

Wolf nodded. There was nothing to say.

"Holy man," Sees spoke again, "what *can* be done? My heart is heavy for the People. Our warriors, who fear nothing, are afraid because they are unable to fight this."

"I understand, my friend. I will talk to my father again."

Wolf left the lodge, nodding a special look of understanding toward young Crow. He made his way back across the camp, the hushed buzz of excitement and fear ringing in his ears, mingling with the rising and falling cadences of the Song of Mourning.

If he had expected his father to provide any answers, he was doomed to disappointment. Walks in the Sun sat in front of the lodge, leaning on his willow backrest. In his hand was his pipe, cold and unheeded. Wolf was shocked to see that the expression on his father's face was much like that of the tracker. There was a reflection of hopelessness there. A hopelessness that he felt himself. It was a frightening thing to see. Two of the strongest and bravest men that he knew were reduced to helplessness over this. Surely there was something . . .

Wolf nodded a greeting to his mother, and sat down beside his father. Walks in the Sun gave a slight nod and a glance that acknowledged his presence, and then resumed his staring into the darkness. Wolf recognized with some degree of surprise that his father looked old. He had never realized that before. Or maybe, he now thought, his father had never *looked* old. The holy man seemed to be aging before his eyes.

Aiee! Was this bear to destroy *everything?* The courage of the People, the bravery of their men, the very lives of the Southern band, one person at a time?

Here was his father, perhaps the most respected man in the entire Elk-dog Nation. It had been Walks in the Sun who led the survivors back from a disastrous southern expedition before Wolf was born. They had faced untold hardships, unknown spirits, and strange creatures, and he had overcome them all. Now he sat here before his lodge, helpless in the face of this threat, old and tired.

Not really so old, thought Wolf. *There are older men among the People. But his spirit weakens.*

Finally, when his father did not speak, Wolf broke the silence.

"*Ah-koh*, Father."

It was a very formal greeting, but Wolf did not feel that a less formal address would be appropriate. It was a serious time.

"*Ah-koh*, Wolf."

"Father, I am made to think that something must be done."

The older man looked at him listlessly.

"But what, Wolf?"

"I do not know. Let us talk of it."

Walks in the Sun nodded, still apathetic. "But talk does nothing."

"That is true, Father. But there must be some way. Your medicine is most powerful. Can you not . . . ?"

"No, no, my son. You know that. Such a gift can never be used to break a taboo."

"Yes, I know, Father. But I thought there

might be some other way. Around the Covenant, instead of breaking it."

The slightest flicker of interest showed for an instant in the old man's eyes.

"What do you mean?"

"I do not know, Father. But there are those in the stories . . . Rabbit sometimes fools Bear, does he not? And Magpie?"

Walks in the Sun appeared to think deeply for a moment, and then Wolf saw his face fall again.

"But those are the Creation stories, Wolf. Rabbit and Magpie are spirit-creatures."

"Is not Bear, also?"

"Well, yes . . ."

"But the People made the Covenant with Bear."

"Yes. But those were First People. They were different from us, maybe. They talked to animals. It was when animals and man all spoke the same tongue."

"But Father, might not Rabbit have some trick that could be used by us?"

The holy man thought some more.

"No," he said slowly. "You are thinking of Rabbit's tricks. Like when he stole fat from Bear while Bear slept. But Rabbit does not steal fat from Bear now. That was at Creation. Nothing that happened then can be changed now.

Like the Covenant. You cannot change that, Wolf, and that is what you are trying to do."

It was terribly frustrating to the younger man to have one trail after another forbidden to him. Yet he knew that there was probably no one who understood these things of the spirit as well as his father.

"Father," he asked, "is this a spirit-bear that causes us to be in mourning?"

"I do not know, my son. It does not matter, does it? We cannot deal with it any differently, because the Covenant is with both the spirit and the animal."

Aiee, thought Wolf, another door closes. He rose to go.

"I have talked to Sees," he said. "We will go out after daylight to see if we can find anything."

His father nodded agreement, but no comment was needed.

"Father," Wolf said desperately, "do you still believe that though this bear is killing us, breaking the Covenant, we must not harm it?"

"I *know* this! He who does will die."

"But this is not fair!" blurted Wolf, childlike in his protest.

Walks in the Sun smiled.

"No one says the world is fair, my son. But you are growing in your thoughts. It is good. We will talk again."

This last was completely confusing to Wolf. Just when he felt more lack of understanding than he had ever had, his father was complimenting him on his thinking. *Aiee!*

"It is good," he mumbled as he turned away toward his own lodge.

The children were sleeping, exhausted by a long hard day and by the excitement of the night. He glanced up at the Seven Hunters and saw that their circuit around the Real-Star indicated it was past midnight. He sat down next to Rain.

"Do you want to eat?" she asked.

"No, I think not. How are the children?" he asked.

"Tired. They do not understand."

"*Aiee! I* do not understand!"

"Nor do I. You talked with your father?"

"Yes. He worries me, Rain. I think his spirit is weakening. He seems to think there is nothing we can do."

"Did you talk to him of the stories of Rabbit?"

"Yes. He says that they do not apply here."

"But Wolf, Rabbit plays tricks on Bear while he sleeps or eats."

"That is true. But I am not Rabbit," he said curtly.

"Maybe, though, we could give Bear our meat as a gift and while he eats, we leave?"

This was a variation on one of Wolf's thoughts, combining the Creation stories with the practicality of today. Maybe . . .

"But my father says *nothing* will work."

"Something *must*, Wolf. Look at the children there. Is there no future for them?"

He looked at the sleeping children and knew that there must be some answer, if he could only find it.

"What are the People saying?" he asked his wife.

"There is much rumor," Rain answered. "A bear in every shadow, of course. Most want to move. You have talked to Sees?"

"Yes. Rain, he is very discouraged . . . afraid. We will go out in the morning, but I am made to think it will do little good."

They sat together in the darkness for a long time, not talking, their closeness a comfort to each other. It was unnecessary to speak.

A young man paused before their lodge.

"Singing Wolf?" he asked.

"Yes . . . what is it?"

"I have been asked to tell you there will be a council in the morning."

Wolf nodded, a bit confused. He had never been personally notified of a council before. Was this something special?

"It is good," he mumbled.

"Now, Broken Lance would speak with you."

Nervously, Wolf followed the young man through the dark village, among the lodges, until they stopped before the big lodge of the band chieftain.

"*Ah-koh*, Wolf," the old man greeted.

"*Ah-koh*, my chief."

The messenger slipped away quietly.

"Sit," offered Broken Lance.

Singing Wolf sat, confused. Why would he be summoned this way in the middle of the night?

"I would speak with you of the real-bear." The chief came immediately to the point.

"I . . . why me, Uncle?" Wolf blurted.

Broken Lance was direct, a quality well recognized by the People.

"You have thought much of this," the old man said. It was a statement, not a question.

"Yes . . . It has troubled me. But my father—"

"Yes, yes. Your father is my friend, and a great holy man, Wolf. But he is like me . . . old. I am made to think he is hopeless about this."

Wolf was astonished. This wise old man, much older than his father, seemed to understand how everyone *felt*, what they thought.

"I have talked with him, Wolf," Broken

Lance went on, partially answering the questions that whirled in Wolf's mind. "He says there is nothing we can do."

"That is true, Uncle. He told me the same."

"But you are not convinced." Again, it was a statement.

"I . . . I do not know, Uncle."

"Good. Many young men will not admit that."

"But, my chief," Wolf protested, "I am inexperienced. All that I know of my medicine I learned from Walks in the Sun."

"Yes, yes. But you think, also. I am made to think, my son, that you will be as great a holy man as he."

Wolf was overwhelmed. It was not right, he thought, for this experienced leader to approach him rather than the older holy man of the band. Yet Broken Lance had said that he *had* consulted with Walks in the Sun.

"Your father says," the chief went on, "that you have some thoughts about this bear. Something about Rabbit?"

Aiee, thought Wolf. *My father seemed to reject that.*

"What are your thoughts?" demanded the old man.

Wolf hesitated.

"My thoughts are not clear, Uncle," he admitted. "I only recalled to my father that in the Creation stories it is sometimes possible to fool Bear. When Bear is occupied with sleep or food, Rabbit or Magpie sometimes steals from him. But my father says that is not the same."

A look of surprise washed over the face of Broken Lance and was gone again.

"He did? *Aiee*, maybe your father is not sure!" He sat thinking for a moment.

Wolf thought of Rain's remark at their lodge a little earlier. A gift to Bear . . .

"Uncle," he said. "My wife and I were talking of this. What if we take what meat we can, leave a fine gift of meat for Bear and his friends . . . Coyote, Buzzard, Wolf. Then leave, while they feast. In the stories, Magpie did something like this once, did he not?"

Broken Lance was deep in thought. It was not necessary to retell the story: Bear, full from feasting, fell sound asleep and Magpie stole some of his beads and trinkets.

"I am made to think this is worth a try," the chief said. "We can hunt again. But this is our chance. We will leave tomorrow."

19

»»»

It may have been the shortest council ever. The urgency of the occasion was plain to all. There was some grumbling about the wasting of good meat, but not much.

As one woman said, "We can get more meat, but lives are scarce."

Once again, the helplessness of any other action was thrust upon them, and the People were ready to move. It would be doubly hard to pack, strike the lodges, and be on the trail while yet attempting to salvage what meat they could. No one spoke of the obvious fact that if a second fall hunt proved unsuccessful, it would be a winter of hunger. For now, they were alive.

This was a short day of travel, but extremely hard. It was no more than mid-morning when the caravan began to form up and move southward. The council had taken little time to agree that they would head south, then veer southeast toward the scrub oak thickets that offered good winter camps.

Singing Wolf and Sees brought up the rear, wolves to protect the last of the column. Again, there were few stragglers. No one wanted to be the last family on the trail. Wolf looked back toward the area of the hunt. They could hear distant sounds of quarreling coyotes at the kills, and the sky seemed full of gathering vultures.

"Eat well, my brothers," he said. "Our misfortune has come to be your good luck!"

He turned his mare and rode on. The two stopped often to watch the back trail. This, of course, was their function as rearguard wolves, but today it held special significance. They wished to be aware of the slightest hint that they were followed. It would be the most important part of this migration, and would determine the success of the effort.

In spite of this importance, neither man mentioned it until after midday.

"I have seen nothing, Wolf," said Sees tentatively. "You?"

"No," Wolf answered cautiously. "Maybe . . ."

He went no further. It was as if the very mention of the threat would continue to make it real. But there comes a time when such a thing must be brought into discussion, to relieve the pressure on the spirit.

"Maybe this time we are successful," suggested Sees cautiously.

Wolf nodded. "Maybe. I am made to think this is the best chance we have had. But let us not be too sure yet."

"Of course, Wolf. Tell me . . . Do you think this is a spirit-bear?"

"I do not know. Does it matter? It is real, and very dangerous. We cannot even try to stop it because of the Covenant, so we must use our wits."

"Why do you think this has happened to the People?" Sees asked.

Wolf shook his head.

"I do not know, my friend. My father says that I try too hard to understand, that it is not meant to be understood. Maybe the spirit-grandfathers are trying to get our attention to tell us something else. Who knows? Or maybe it is as we have thought before. This is only a bear who has gone mad and broken the Covenant. If that is it, this will be equaled out sometime. But I think we are not yet meant to know."

It was a long speech for the usually quiet Wolf, but he felt better. Maybe he was only thinking out loud. A new idea was creeping into his thought, and this was the first time it had found voice. He turned it over again in his mind.

The idea which had seemed to occur to him even as he spoke a moment ago . . . What if his spirit-guides *were* trying to get his attention? Was there something that he was being called to do, but had not yet heard the call? If so, *what?*

He remembered, as they remounted now after the brief rest stop, that he had had trouble before when listening for the spirits. He had been older than most before he had received the call and the gift as a holy man. Even then, he had fought it a little. He did not refuse the gift, though he could have if he did not wish the responsibility. But his thoughts had been on other things. He had been among the first to have and use one of the French thundersticks. He felt that was important. He had become one of the most skilled in the band in the use of the thunderstick's black powder, and its ability to deliver a lethal blow at a great distance.

He carried the thunderstick now, in its beaded case. He had actually used it seldom in recent years. He was more occupied now with his role as a holy man. With things of the spirit. Less with the things of the hunt, the contests, the warrior skills. How long since he had fired the musket? He could not remember. He should probably fire it and clean it. But not now.

He rode on, still wondering about things of the spirit. Was this another instance where he was not paying attention to the spirit-call? Was he supposed to be getting some sort of message here? Was Wolf himself somehow the answer to this year of trouble for the People?

It was incredible to him as he thought back, that he had been so closely involved since the first. He had been concerned when his father, even with all his skills, had missed the importance of the first kill. Yet Wolf, with his constant feeling of the bear's significance to him and to the People, had never even seen it. But was he even now fulfilling the spirit-call? Had he been led to talk to the band chief, and been responsible for the decision that now had the band on the move?

He liked that idea. Maybe that *was* it. He had been quietly readied for this behind-the-scenes leadership role in the major decision to make this move away from the danger. It was good!

Thank you, Grandfather, he prayed silently. Then another thought occurred to him. Maybe he had been too preoccupied with other things. Day-to-day chores, his wife and children, the problems of those who came to him for the benefits of his medicine. *Let me listen well, Grandfather,* he went on. *If I am meant to learn more, help me be ready.*

Their winter camp came a bit early because of their disruptive season. It was in an area of mixed grassland and scrub oaks. These would be valuable as shelter because they hold their leaves until well past the Moon of Snows. It was a familiar area to the Southern band, and this gave them a sense of security.

Even better, there was no sign of the bear. It began to be accepted that the gift of meat and the swift retreat had evened the score, and that things would now revert to normal. Life was good.

It was a pleasant Second Summer, and as it happened, meat was plentiful. There was no second fall hunt, but there seemed to be a constant trickle of small bands of buffalo, from which a few animals were harvested at a time.

"Aiee, this is better than the fall hunt," chuckled one old woman. "The work does not come all at once!"

And, even better, normal-acting black bears were seen often, scavenging the leavings of the kills. The People were uneasy at first, but there was no sign of real-bears. They began to relax. Maybe the Covenant was restored.

A moon passed, and another. With each passing day, Singing Wolf gained confidence that it was really over at last. Life was good again. He gathered plants and herbs for his use through the winter. Here, also, were many of those used for smoking. Sumac, catnip, grape, and a few leaves of cedar, to be mixed with corn silks and tobacco. Traders should be along soon with tobacco. Wolf hoped that they would also carry sweetgrass from the northern plains. The nations who lived there used it, he had heard, along with sage, to call the attention of the spirits. He liked its incense, and if it could appease the spirits or catch their attention, so much the better. One could always use better communication with the spirits, no? It had taken him much too long to understand his part in this thing of the bear and the Covenant.

This particular afternoon Wolf was seated in front of the lodge, leaning comfortably on his backrest and smoking in the sunlight. For once, all of the household chores were completed. Rain sat with him. The children were playing at the stream, with a number of others. They could hear the childish laughter. It was a good day to be alive.

"It is good to hear the laughter," said Rain. "It has been a long time."

This was her way of saying that it was over, he thought.

"Yes. It is good."

"Even Sees is more like himself," Rain

went on. "He passed by here this morning, and was much as we remember him, before the . . ." She paused.

"Before the bear?" he suggested.

"Yes . . . You do not think it bad luck to speak of it? Wolf, it *is* over, is it not?"

"I am made to think so. Everything has to end, even that. *Aiee*, what a fearful year! But let us not speak of it, Rain. How is our lodge supplied for winter?"

"It is good. The meat on the rack there is the last. It should be more than enough."

"You will make more pemmican?"

"Maybe. I think we will store this dry, though. I can grind it later if we want to."

It was merely a topic of conversation for a lazy afternoon. There was nothing urgent. They were comfortable with each other and with the day.

"I am happy with you, my husband," Rain said suddenly.

"*Aiee!*" he teased. "You are not sorry that you did not marry that young man from the Eastern band? What was his name?"

She made a face at him.

"Do I look like a woman who would marry into the Eastern band?" she demanded. Then she became serious. "That was never really a risk, you know, Wolf."

"Then my heart is good," he said, reaching for her hand.

The interlude was interrupted by a sudden change in the voices of the children at the stream. Shouts of laughter changed to screams of terror. They jumped to their feet, and Wolf was sprinting in that direction. Close behind came Rain. She had paused to snatch a lance from the weapons rack in front of the lodge.

Frightened children were running away from the stream, still screaming. Other adults, weapons in hand, ran toward the area, shouting questions.

Now Wolf saw Dawn and Dark Antelope running to meet them in panic. Dawn was screaming, Antelope crying. He saw no sign of Little Owl.

"Where is Owl?" he cried as Dawn swept into his arms.

"Father, Father," the girl screamed. "Owl is gone! A huge bear came out of the thicket and carried him away!"

20

》》》

Little Owl. Even with all of the emotion of the past year, Singing Wolf was totally unprepared for this loss. Until now, his concern had been primarily for the People as a group. Danger from the bear had been something that was a threat to others. Not to his own family.

And Owl . . . *aiee*, the hurt of it!

One cannot choose a favorite among his children. One is loved for his quiet humor, another for her sensitive sympathy for others. Still another for her zest for life, and the way that she makes every common incident exciting.

Owl had been the quiet and thoughtful one, easygoing and pleased with the world. Wolf suspected that Owl was the one who would be offered the spirit-gifts of his father and grandfather. In many ways the child reminded him of Walks in the Sun. His way of walking, his serious manner, yet with underlying good humor. In other ways the child reminded Wolf of himself as a child. Owl would spend long periods watching an ant heap.

"What are you doing, Owl?"

"I am watching the ant people, Father. See, it is their fall hunt."

The boy would point to the column of ants, busily dismembering and carrying off bits of a large grasshopper.

"They carry the meat to their lodge," Owl explained solemnly.

Such understanding, in one so young! thought Wolf. Then they would talk of such things, and the way of birds and snakes and the seasons and the buffalo. Talking with Little Owl was much like visiting with an adult.

Owl was aptly named. It was a name that had been obvious from the time of his birth. He had opened his eyes to stare around at the new world in which he had just arrived. The serious stare, like that of an old man, had seemed amusing. From that moment, he was the Owl, or Little Owl.

"An ancestor of ours carried that name," Wolf told his wife. "He was a great holy man."

"It is good," Rain had answered. "Maybe this one will be, also."

But now it was over, their pride in this,

their youngest. Their baby . . . though Owl
did not like to be designated so. It was somehow beneath his dignity, even as a child. It did
not matter now, Wolf told himself. It was finished. The spirit, this all-knowing and all-
understanding spirit that had brought them
such joy as parents, was gone. Owl had crossed
over, amid tragic events. There was an empty
place in the lodge, and in their hearts. The Song
of Mourning had never carried such significance. Wolf was glad, in a perverse way, to be
able to throw back his head and cry out in his
pain. There was relief to be found in the out-
pouring of grief. He and Rain shared their loss,
clinging together like lost children as they
mourned together.

There had been no trace found of the child,
except a moccasin and a few drops of blood. It
was clean and quick, it seemed, and for that
Wolf was grateful. The first adults to arrive at
the scene of the attack had found the pitiful
little shoe at the water's edge. The tracker,
with some recovery of his old confidence, had
identified the blood trail.

"Moving fast," Sees pointed out. "See, a
drop, with a spatter of droplets pointing that
way."

It was a gruesome thing, a hurtful thing for
Wolf, but necessary. He must know, and not
hold hope where there was none.

"And it is the same, the scar-footed bear?" he asked. He already knew the answer.

"Yes," the tracker said. "A track, at the stream, there. My heart is heavy for you, my friend."

Now a great weight of guilt descended upon Wolf. *I should have known!* he told himself repeatedly. *Why did I not!*

He began a great depth of soul-searching. Again he began to explore the events of the season in his mind. There was the nagging thought that from the first, he had overlooked something. He was convinced that he, Wolf, was personally involved with this bear. There was something . . . the odd feeling returned that somehow the Grandfathers had been trying to get his attention and he had not been listening. This led to more guilt. *Aiee*, had it been necessary to lose a child, their youngest, to catch his attention? And what now? He spent much time in prayer, when not mourning.

"Grandfather," he spoke to his spirit-guide, "may I be forgiven for not listening? But now I *do* listen. What is it that is asked of me? I do not know, but I am ready. What must I do?"

He had begun a fast when Owl was lost. That should sharpen his senses and bring closer contact with the spirits. He shared his mourning with Rain and the other children, but there were thoughts that he could not share, even with Rain. He was searching frantically almost, trying to establish some path of action. Or at least, some path of understanding.

After the first day, he began to feel the keen edge of his sight and hearing honed to near perfection by his fast. He had experienced this before, on his vision quest, and each time he fasted. It was as he had hoped now. He began to see the world with increasing clarity and understanding. The hunger pangs which had been uncomfortable on other occasions of fasting were overshadowed this time by pains of grief. Now even these began to be replaced by the calm brightness of spirit, a clarity that he hoped would lend light to the darkness of his soul.

He had slept not at all on that fearsome first night after Owl's death. On the second, he did not expect to sleep, but found himself drifting in and out of a dreamlike state. It was like being awake yet seeing the visions of a dream. He knew that the pictures in his mind were dream-pictures, but he saw them as a detached observer. These were jumbled and unclear, shifting and changing like the images of fish and other objects seen through rippling water.

There was one image that kept recurring, that of the bear. It was a great grizzled giant of a creature, and it was terrifying to see. It would raise itself to full height, much taller than a man, and would roar in his face. It was so real that he could practically smell its breath.

Then he would waken, wet with a cold sweat, aware that he had drowsed, after all. Mixed with his terror at the clarity of this night-vision were guilt and hurt. He realized that what he was seeing might well have been the last conscious image in Little Owl's life.

Grandfather, what is it, he prayed silently. *What? What must I do?*

Each time the recurring vision was shown to him, his anger rose. It began to replace his guilt. Gradually even that was replaced by acceptance, and by concern. Though it was over for Owl, it now occurred to him that the bear was still a threat to others of the People. Something must be done to stop this cycle of killing. The People would never be safe until that happened. Incongruously, he thought of the grasshopper that Owl had shown him long ago. The Southern band was being dismembered, as the ants had cut apart the insect. It was being carried off, a small piece at a time. A *person* at a time. Eventually, none would be left.

He did not understand why, and did not try. It was only that it was so. And close on the heels of this realization came the other. He, Wolf, must be the one to stop this terrible destruction of an entire band of the People. He had previously felt a hint of this but had denied it. *Aiee*, if he had listened, it might have saved Little Owl.

No matter, now. That was water down the stream. He could not fully share his plans with Rain. He regretted this, because they had always shared their innermost thoughts. But she would understand, later. If he told her now, she would try to stop him. And nothing must stop him now.

Wolf rose with the sun, and went to the rise to the east of the camp. He did not even look to see if there was danger. He was above and beyond that.

"I am ready, Grandfather!" he prayed aloud. "Help me do what I must."

He stood there, bathed in the glowing rays of the rising sun, and a peace came over him, peace and recognition of his duty. He was now free to make his plans.

He would tell no one, even Rain, about the goal that he had set for himself. To tell that would force him to try to justify what he intended to do, and that would be difficult. No, he would tell his wife that he had a plan to save the People from the bear. It would require fasting and prayer, much like a vision quest. He would explain that it involved his gifts and

that he would be using a special medicine to
end the threat that had hung over them for a
year.

All of this was true, and he felt that he
must be as truthful with Rain as he could. He
had never lied to her, and would not now.
He would tell her that he would be gone for a
few days, to deal with this emergency that
called upon his gifts and his skills. This, too,
would be true. He would simply not tell her *all*
of the truths that he knew.

He turned back toward the camp, excited
in the knowledge that now he *could* do something. It was stimulating, in an odd way. But he
had much to do today, preparations to make.
He thought of going to talk to his father, but
rejected the idea. The less *anyone* knew about
this, the better.

Rain was at the lodge fire, her hair fouled
with ashes in mourning for her lost child.
There was dried blood on her arms from the
gashes she had inflicted on herself in the ritual.
Even so, she must look after the needs of her
other children. Then she would raise again the
Song of Mourning.

He told her what he could of his plans, and
she nodded. Rain was distracted by her loss,
and he wondered whether she had really heard
him.

Wolf took down the thunderstick and removed it from its beaded case. He did not wish to fire it now. Somehow that would be inappropriate. But it was essential to his plan that it be functional. He checked the screw-tip on the ramrod, and inserted it down the weapon's mouth to draw the lead ball out and empty the load. A fresh charge of the black medicine-powder . . .

"You will use the thunderstick on this vision quest?" Rain demanded.

He looked up to see her staring at him, wide-eyed. Maybe she knew more than he realized.

"*Aiee*, I must protect myself! One does not go unarmed!" he told her.

Rain appeared unconvinced, but let the matter drop. He finished cleaning the weapon, and changed the flint for a new one. Then he reloaded, using carefully chosen components, powder, patch, and ball.

"When will you return?" his wife asked, her voice flat.

"I do not know . . . a few days. However long it takes."

He hugged each of the children, and then his wife, kissing her gently.

"Do you not want food?" she asked.

"No. I am fasting until this is over."

"Ah, yes. You told me. You will be care-ful?"

"Of course, Rain."

He slipped the beaded case back on his gun, and stooped to leave the lodge.

21

>> >> >>

Wolf's quest began at the stream where the tragedy had occurred. He spent a short while there in devout prayer, then rose and crossed the riffle at the gravel bar. His heart was heavy as he wondered just where . . . It did not matter now.

He glanced aside only for a moment at the area where the tracks had been found. It was not necessary to look for what he already knew. More important was a general direction, and he had an idea of that from the findings of the tracker.

It might have been helpful to talk to Sees again. The tracker's instincts were good, and he might have given valuable suggestions. But Wolf decided not to ask. His friend would surely question Wolf's purpose and realize what was planned. Hopefully, no one would know until it was too late to interfere.

He would have liked to talk to his father, too. That would have been a comfort. Yet he doubted that Walks in the Sun would understand. It was easier to begin this, the most important quest of his life, without the knowledge of his father. Wolf did not think that he could have defied his father to proceed with what he must do.

No, in this he was alone. The most hurtful part was that he had thought it necessary to deceive his wife. For that his heart was heavy. He was certain that after it was over she would understand. Did she not always understand? There would be a time when she thought otherwise, but after . . . *Aiee*, he must not dwell on such thoughts! He shook them off and moved up the slope. He must concentrate on his mission, and use all his senses most keenly.

Out of sight of the camp, he stopped to orient himself to the terrain. Again he envied the skills of the tracker. But, he told himself earnestly, any deficiency would be overcome by his fasting, his dedication, and the importance of his decision for the good of the People.

First he must find the bear. From the knoll where he stood, he could see the winter camp of the People, the lodges scattered among the sheltering oak thickets. The stream wandered past, and beyond to the east was the camp of the New band.

From the angle of the attack at the stream, he must decide the path the bear might have taken. Sees had indicated the direction in which the animal had retreated after the kill . . . ah, how that thought stuck in his throat! It was like ashes on his tongue. He must rise above this, he knew. He would try to think like the bear, to put his spirit inside the bear's head, to think as the bear did.

With this, he began to see certain things. The direction of the wind, the likeliest area in which a bear might be concealed. At this season, the bear would be in the process of selecting a place for the winter sleep, would he not? Wolf looked at the features of the land a little farther from the camp. Yes, now it was becoming clear . . . The scrub oaks in the immediate area offered temporary concealment, but the bear would need heavier timber for his winter lodge.

Wolf's attention was drawn to a rocky ridge in the distance. Yes, that was the only place in sight that offered what the bear would need. Shelter, concealment, timber, large jumbled rocks. The location was even such that the prevailing wind currents were in the bear's favor. Why had he not noticed this before?

The answer, of course, was quite obvious. The People had never hunted bears. There had been no occasion for them to notice such things. Their way demanded that they know in detail the habits of buffalo, elk, and deer. But not bears. Bears were to be avoided, to be left alone, not to be hunted.

Until now. Now there would be a change. At least temporarily, at least for this one individual. This bear would be held to answer for having broken the Covenant. Wolf shifted the robe over his shoulder, and started toward the distant ridge.

He had elected to go on foot for this quest. A horse would have been easier, but he had realized that he would not have far to travel. His quarry must be nearby. In this elemental contest, it seemed appropriate not to encumber the face-off any more than necessary. A horse would be a distraction, and there was no place for any distractions. There was only one purpose, one thought in Wolf's mind.

I am coming, Bear.

He crossed the valley, skirting around islands of brushy growth that dotted the grassy expanse. While they might afford hiding for a bear, it would be temporary. *And I must meet him where he lives,* Wolf thought.

Straight on toward the ridge he traveled. He paused, searched the slopes above him with a glance, and selected the place he would go. A high rock, perched like a sentry at the crest of the ridge. From there he could see the entire valley, and also overlook most of the south slope of the rocky ridge itself. From there, he would watch.

It took much of the afternoon to reach the rock. It was harder than he expected, the climb up the slope. In some places his progress was impeded by thick growth, in others by the jumbled piles of stone. *It is good*, he thought. *If I were a bear, I would winter here.*

Finally, when he drew himself up and stood on the overlook, the sun was low in the west. The view was as he had hoped. From here he could see any moving thing for a long distance. Half a day, maybe. With an unexpected shiver, he realized that quite possibly his own movement across the valley and up the ridge had been observed by the great bear. It could even now be planning to stalk him. Would he be the hunter or the hunted?

He shook off that thought, and turned his attention to the examination of the slope. His own present location should be relatively safe. It would not be easy for the bear to climb the rock without warning. So he passed the time that remained before dark by studying the terrain, making himself familiar with every feature. He must know all that lay before him as well as he knew the palm of his hand.

In the distance there, a gray smudge of smoke indicated the camp of the People. Closer to him, a band of elk grazed undisturbed. On the front slope of the timbered ridge where he now stood, he tried to visualize areas that were likely places for a bear's winter den. There were three, he decided. One was a tumble of large square stones, debris from the crumbling of a rocky shelf. Another was a cleft in the face of the ridge, sheltered and heavily timbered. The third was a tangle of downed timber on a steep portion of the slope. It could have been caused by a severe windstorm, or by the weight of ice in a freak spring storm. Regardless of the cause, it was a possible shelter for the bear. The animal could be in any of the three places. He would watch and wait.

He drew his robe around him against the chill that came with the fading of Sun Boy's torch. It was also a bit chilling to realize that even now, Bear was probably watching him.

As darkness fell, Rain was troubled. She tried to go about the household tasks of the lodge, but it was hard. She was still mourning for her lost child, yet had to look after the other two also, and attend to their needs.

On top of all this, she was worried about her husband. Wolf had acted very strangely. He had explained that this mysterious quest had to do with his medicine-gifts. She knew that often matters pertaining to the gifts of the holy man

could not be discussed, and she had always accepted that. But this time, something was different. The distraction of her grief and her
preoccupation had interfered with her understanding, but now she looked back at their last
conversation. *Aiee,* she should have known
what he was planning! He was fasting, as if for
a vision quest, so he had taken no food. She
was not certain, but as nearly as she could recall, he had taken very little that would have to
do with the skills of his gifts as a holy man.

What he *had* carried was the thunderstick.
Now she recalled that he had spent much time
in the cleaning, preparation, and reloading of
the weapon. He had been quite vague about his
mission, but now it was becoming clearer to
her. He had said, or at least had implied that he
had a plan, and that it involved his medicine. It
had not even occurred to her, the significance
of the way that he said it. He had even said
casually that the weapon was for defense. In
her preoccupation, she had not questioned it.

Now she realized that he had spoken truth.
He always did that, but this time she was made
to think that it was not the entire truth. Wolf
was carrying his thunderstick for a specific
purpose, and she was afraid that she knew that
purpose. But surely it could not be. Wolf would
not consider breaking the Covenant.

She tucked the children into their sleeping-robes and straightened again.

"I am going to the lodge of your grandparents for a little while," she told them. "You must stay in bed."

She slipped through the doorway and into the night. It was not far to the lodge of Deer and Walks in the Sun. She tapped on the lodge skin.

"Uncle," she called, "it is Rain. I would speak with you."

The door skin lifted and Walks in the Sun emerged.

"What is it, almost-daughter?"

"I . . . Maybe I should not have come," she stammered, embarrassed.

"Yes, if there is something that is needed," he said.

"But I . . . Did Wolf speak to you before he left?"

"He *left?* Where? When?"

"I do not know, Uncle. He left earlier in the day. He spoke of fasting and a quest. He did not tell you?"

"No. I know nothing of this, Rain. He did not say where?"

"No, Uncle. He said he would be gone a few days."

"And he took no food?"

"That is true. He was fasting."

"What *did* he take?"

"I am not sure, Uncle. A little tobacco, maybe. His thunderstick, and the powder for it."

Walks in the Sun appeared startled.

"His *musket?*"

"Yes. He unloaded and cleaned it. He said, to defend himself. But he was planning a ceremony. At least, I think that is what he said. One to stop the trouble with the bear who causes our mourning."

"*Aiee!*" muttered Walks in the Sun softly.

"Uncle," Rain pushed on, "I am made to think now that he means to kill the bear."

"And I am made to think you may be right," the holy man observed. "Daughter, this is very bad."

"The Covenant?"

"Yes. Rain, if we are right, and if this is what he plans, he will die."

"From the bear? It will kill him?"

"Maybe. The means may vary. But he will surely die from the breaking of the Covenant of the Bear."

"Can we not stop him?"

"I think not. This is for him to choose, daughter. *Aiee*, so much sorrow!"

22

»»»

Wolf did not sleep. He was too engrossed with his plan. He sat or lay on the rock and watched the Seven Hunters circle overhead through the night. His senses were tightly tuned to the sounds of the night-creatures by the clarity of fasting. Occasionally he sipped a little water from his waterskin. A time or two he heard a large creature moving on the slopes below him. But then there would be nothing.

An owl sailed silently across the sky above him, blotting out a patch of stars for a moment as it passed.

Good hunting to you, Grandfather, he thought.

With the first yellowing of dawn he was up, searching for any sign of movement below. At first there was nothing, but then he heard the alarm call of a crow, and shifted his glance in that direction. Surely . . . Yes! A flicker of motion among the brown of the oaks. A patch of lighter color, perhaps. He focused on that area as the light grew stronger. Then the moving figure came into full view in a small clearing between the brushy trees. Wolf sat frozen in amazement at the size of the creature, a gigantic bear, the grizzled real-bear. Surely, the grandfather of all bears.

He sat staring as it moved along a dim trail among the oaks, now visible, now hidden. It would have been within easy range of the thunderstick, but the weapon lay forgotten in his lap. His body was covered with cold sweat, and his palms were wet. How could he have thought . . . But yes, he *must*. Stealthily, he reached for the thunderstick, but the bear had disappeared in a tangle below him. For a moment he was disappointed, but then a sense of elation came over him. He was on the right trail. He had successfully gotten into the bear's thinking, and had maneuvered into a favorable position. Yes, from here he could see the path that the bear had been following. He was sure that the tangled windfall into which it had disappeared must be its lair. Now he had only to watch and wait. The next time the animal revealed itself he would not be hampered by the shock and surprise. He would be ready. He was certain that he could make the leaden ball fly true, even though it had been a long time since he fired the gun.

He relaxed, pleased with himself. He could hardly wait. He even considered going down to follow the path straight to the bear's den. But no, that was too risky. He did not want to play the hero. The shot from ambush was better, more sure. The result was to be the same anyway, as he understood the teachings of his father. The result for him, Wolf, that is.

Wolf ran the whole thing through his mind once more. If he was unsuccessful in killing the bear with his first shot, he would still be in violation of the Covenant. He would be in great danger if he only wounded the bear. But either way, he could expect the certain punishment for breaking the pact . . . Death. If his leaden ball flew true, of course, the bear would no longer trouble the People. He, Wolf, having violated the Covenant, would not be there to see their relief, their happiness that at last it was over.

That bothered him a little, but he drew great satisfaction from the thought that in dying, he would have done so for a greater good. He regretted that he must do this thing, but his regret was personal. He did not like to think that he would not be there for his children as they grew up. He would not see Dawn marry and set up her own lodge. He would not be there to take part in Dark Antelope's initiation into one of the warrior societies. At this point he became misty-eyed. Little Owl . . . *aiee,* the pain would return as long as he lived. Maybe after. Then he reassured himself that the action he would take today or tomorrow was to assure that his children *would* grow up, and not fall to the same tragedy that had taken Owl. And in that way it was good. They could grow up untroubled by the threat of this bear, which seemed completely unrestricted by the rules of the Covenant.

He still did not understand that part. He had found no answer to his questions about the bear. Was it a spirit-creature or merely a large real-bear with some sort of madness? He did not know, and might never learn. In fact, he probably had little time left to learn anything.

There was one thing that brought him deep sorrow as he pondered the events to come. He hated to inflict the pain on his wife. Rain was the sweetheart of his childhood, the woman of his dreams as a young man. And as he had come to maturity, she had been a warm and loving wife, a helpmate in his late-coming tasks as a holy man.

Yes, he regretted that he had felt it necessary to deceive her. His death would hurt her, especially so soon after the loss of their child. But he hoped to avoid for her the greater hurt

and the terror of living under the threat of the
bear, and its threat to her other children. He
did not relish the idea of Rain as the wife of
another man, but he realized that it was likely
she would remarry. It was the way of things.
She would be eligible, and was still young and
attractive. He hoped that her life would be
good, and that she would understand when she
realized what he had done. It was important
that she understand. He wished that their
goodbye had been more satisfactory.

By this time, Wolf had convinced himself
that this was a personal thing on the part of the
real-bear. Maybe in his grief Wolf had gone a
little mad. He admitted this possibility to himself. It was not purely in the interests of the
People that he now intended to kill the bear. It
was in part the desire to avenge the death of his
son. So it was a double purpose that drove him
to the act that he now intended. Vengeance, as
well as a better life for the Southern band. His
life would be well given for this.

He wondered some about the manner of
his death. He had not dared to inquire any
more about it after he conceived this plan. But
earlier, he had understood his father to say that
the manner of the punishment for the broken
Covenant might have nothing to do with the
act that broke it. So, if he killed this bear—no,
when he killed it—he might be killed by the

bear itself in its dying struggle, or from accident or illness later. It might be good to have a little time. Maybe he would be permitted to see Rain once again before . . .

No, he hoped not. That would be too difficult. Tears came to his eyes at the mere thought of having to admit to her what he had done, and that he would now be doomed. He shook off the thought. He must be alert now, not lost in such distractions. But *aiee*, how he wished there had been time, time to hold her in his arms a little longer.

Wolf spent the day in such troubling thoughts, alternately depressed and almost joyful in the knowledge that it was nearly over. He had resolved not to sleep, but he must have done so. He came suddenly awake in the late afternoon, unsure where he was, and troubled at his inattention. Sun Boy was somewhat farther down the sky than Wolf had realized, so he must have slept.

Below him somewhere, a crow sounded its alarm. A deer went leaping through the oak thickets, noisier than deer usually are. It must have been alarmed. Instantly, all his attention was focused on the area of the windfall. He reached for the thunderstick, checking the priming powder in the pan. He placed his powder horn on the rock before him, and rolled out a couple of bullets. He wanted to be ready to reload, though reason told him that there would be only one shot, one way or another.

He studied the terrain, and reviewed the meandering path where he had seen the bear before. If it came out again and passed this way, his best shot would be in a little clearing directly below him. It would be no more than fifty paces. Surely a target the size of the real-bear would be hard to miss. He wondered what would be most effective. A head shot? Or should he try for the chest cavity, the heart or lungs, as one would when the quarry was a buffalo? An easier shot . . . Maybe he should wait and see what presented.

Even as he settled himself in a comfortable sitting position from which to shoot, Wolf was watching the stretch of the path nearest the windfall. That *must* be the bear's lodge, he told himself. But he saw nothing, and began to doubt. Had he missed seeing the bear as it left the den? Was there another trail?

It could be possible, even, that whatever startled the deer had not been the bear at all, but something else. Or . . . could there be *more than one bear?* He found himself in a cold sweat, and glanced around anxiously, but saw nothing.

Then, a glimpse of motion below, near the windfall. Yes! Even larger than before, the creature appeared. It moved along the path on a course that would again bring it directly past the rock where he sat. Yes, his chosen shot would happen nicely. He carefully moved the gun so that it would point at his target when it arrived there, and tentatively lined up the sights. *Yes, when the bear crosses just past the sycamore, there . . .*

The bear moved closer, slowly, almost lazy in its deliberate advance. It was as if it feared nothing. *And why should it?* thought Wolf. *There is nothing to challenge it.*

"Except now, Bear, *I* am here!" he whispered. "You will never kill again!"

Now that the time was at hand, his tension was gone. He was calm, steady, and confident. There was almost a joy in the thing that he now faced. A triumph, after a year of tragedy and hurt for the People. This, his last act over which he would have any control, would be remembered as Singing Wolf's gift to the People of the Southern band. Deliverance from an enemy that threatened.

The words of the Death Song, the song with which the People rode into battle against hopeless odds, flashed through his mind as he waited:

The sky and the grass go
on forever,

*But today is a good day
to die!*

For the first time he fully understood the heart of the warrior who is determined to give his life for a greater good, to benefit others . . . his loved ones and his People.

23

»»»

Back in the camp that day, the tracker had gone again to express his sympathy to the mourning family of his friend for the loss of their child. He tapped on the lodge skin and asked for Singing Wolf.

"He is not here," explained Rain.

"Not here? Where is he?"

She gestured at random toward the landscape.

"I do not know. Out there somewhere. It is a medicine-quest to stop the bear."

Sees asked a few more questions, but he felt that there was something missing here. It was apparent that his friend's wife knew or suspected more than she was saying. It was not like Wolf to leave his family at the time of mourning. Sees left the lodge of Singing Wolf puzzled and unsatisfied.

This was very strange. A holy man of the Southern band, absent on some mysterious quest. His wife was being somewhat evasive, but maybe she really did not know. Sees hated to bother her further in this, her time of grief.

Sees tried to remember the conversations that he had had with Singing Wolf. Wolf had always denied that his medicine could be used against the marauding bear, but now appeared to have a plan. And Walks in the Sun . . . Did he know of Wolf's plan, or was he part of it? It had been Walks in the Sun who had repeatedly told Wolf that there was nothing that the medicine of either of them could do.

But now . . . Sees furrowed his brow in thought. It was much easier to read sign than to try to think through such things. Yet, in a way, it was much the same. He walked out of the camp a little way, to think better without the distraction of the camp's noise.

Singing Wolf must have a plan for the use of his medicine to stop the bear. That was the business of holy men, but Sees was a little surprised that Wolf had said nothing to him. They had become close confidants over this problem of the bear. For Wolf not to tell him that he had discovered a way seemed strange. Sees was also made to think that Wolf had not let his father know.

Suddenly it came to him. *Aiee!* Singing

Wolf had gone to *kill* the bear! Knowing that it would mean his own death . . . Of course! *That* would explain why he had told no one. It was likely that any of his friends or family would try to stop him. And rightly so, for Wolf was traveling a trail that was virtual suicide! And yet . . .

Sees stood there, feeling helpless. What could he do? The plan of Singing Wolf was becoming clearer in his mind, and he wished that in some way he could help. He went to talk to the horse herders, and learned that Wolf had not taken a horse. *He is on foot, then.*

Sees went to the gravel bar at the stream, and after some time sorted out enough tracks to put together a theory. Wolf, on foot, had started to follow the trail of the bear toward a distant ridge. Yes, that would be the likeliest place for the bear to make his winter lodge.

The tracker glanced at the sun. The day was late, but he felt an urgency. Quickly, he saddled a horse and hurried toward the ridge. He had no idea what he would do when he got there, but he felt his courage returning, and it was good.

The bear, moving steadily along the trail, now paused. It sniffed the air, swinging its great head from side to side. Wolf could see the nostrils flaring, even at this distance. Or maybe he imagined that he could. The animal was still out of the sure range of his musket.

He sat perfectly still, wondering if the bear was catching *his* scent. He was unsure, but one thing was certain. *Something* was wrong. The bear was being distracted. Wolf's anger rose. Nothing must interfere now!

Anxiously, he wondered if he dared risk a shot at this range. It was far . . . The thought returned that to shoot and only wound would be to fail. If the bear lived and Wolf did not, the situation would be worse than before. He waited, unmoving.

The bear had completely stopped now, still swinging the broad head to catch any hint of something different on the breeze. What could be happening here?

Now the bear seemed to focus its attention on a particular clump of scrub oaks. Something there was causing a distraction. Then, to his complete astonishment, Wolf heard the words of the song that had flashed through his mind a few moments before.

> *The sky and the grass go*
> *on forever . . .*

Its high-pitched wail floated across the slope, unwavering in its determination.

*But today is a good day
to die!*

The bear seemed to locate the source of its confusion, and turned toward the thicket with a determined stride. From the thicket rose the figure of a man, clad in the buckskins of the People, and holding a lance or short spear. He stepped boldly to meet the advance of the bear, still singing.

No! Wolf wanted to shout. *This revenge is mine!* An illogical rage consumed him, and he jumped to his feet, unsure what to do. Then he realized that there was nothing that he *could* do. The scene was unfolding before him, and he was only able to watch.

There was something familiar about the man. Wolf stared, puzzled, as the bear rose to its full height, towering over the figure that confronted it. The bear roared its challenge. Then recognition dawned.

"Father!" screamed Singing Wolf. "No!"

He swung the thunderstick to his shoulder, thumbing back the flint as he did so. He sighted quickly and pulled the trigger. There was a flash in the priming pan and a heartbeat later the weapon boomed, bucking against his shoulder. His vision was obscured by the cottony cloud of smoke, but he knew that he had missed. He cursed himself for aiming too quickly, even as he reached for his powder horn. He was dumping the black powder down the bore when the breeze shifted and the smoke cleared. The scene had actually changed very little. The bear must have paused for a moment in its advance, and then decided that the man below was the greater threat. It moved forward.

Walks in the Sun stepped to meet the attack, his spear ready.

Singing Wolf, trying to reload while watching the scene below, dropped his bullet, felt for another, and lost it, too. But now he was watching the drama develop. It was too late to lend any help now.

Still shrilling the Death Song, the holy man took a long step and swung his spear in an underhand thrust. As nearly as Wolf could tell, the sharp flint point entered the soft underbelly of the bear in the vee of the ribs, just below the chest cavity, thrust with all of Walks in the Sun's wiry strength. The point ranged upward, burying half of the shaft of the spear in the body of the bear.

The bear screamed, and the mighty claws swung. Walks in the Sun was struck by the glancing blow as he ducked aside, and thrown like a rag doll. The bear screamed again and stepped forward, still upright, with the shaft of the spear sticking incongruously out of its belly.

To Wolf in his helplessness, the action seemed to slow. His father lay limply on the ground for a moment while the bear stood over him. Then, like a ponderous tree, the dying creature toppled forward, nearly on top of the limp form of the holy man. The butt of the spear struck the ground, forcing its point grotesquely up, thrusting through the left side of the grizzled back. The bear struggled weakly, kicked a time or two, and was still.

By this time, Wolf had jumped down from his rock and was racing forward, his belt ax in hand. But there was no need for it. The bear was dead.

"Father!" Wolf cried. He dragged the injured Walks in the Sun clear of the bear's limbs, and sat to cradle his father's head in his lap. Tears were streaming down his face.

Walks in the Sun opened his eyes weakly and smiled.

"Why, Father, *why?*" Wolf pleaded.

"I . . . I could not let you do it, Wolf."

"You knew?"

"Yes . . . Rain came to me."

"*She* knew?"

"She was not sure. Wolf, she does not know I came . . ." He paused, coughing weakly, then continued. "Do not let her blame herself."

"No, no, Father. But you should not—"

Walks in the Sun held up his hand.

"Let it go, Wolf. I could not let you do it. I have had a good life, and you have much ahead." He coughed again, and his breath was coming harder. "Oh, yes . . . I think your mother . . . knows . . . what I planned."

"Father, let me help you. You will be—"

"No!" said Walks in the Sun sharply. "You know . . . Wolf . . . the Covenant . . ."

Wolf nodded and his father continued, weakening rapidly now.

"It is over . . . It is even now. Bear has paid and . . . so has Man. The Covenant . . . is . . . even again."

Wolf thought that he was gone, but Walks in the Sun opened his eyes once more.

"I . . . glad you missed . . . thunderstick. Better . . ."

There was a wry smile of triumph on the face of the holy man as he closed his eyes for the last time.

Singing Wolf lifted his face toward the setting sun and his voice in the Song of Mourning.

It was midnight when Wolf heard a horse approaching. He had built a small fire, had straightened his father's limbs in preparation for burial, and now sat in mourning, waiting for daylight.

Sees rode into the circle of firelight and swept the scene with a quick glance. He dismounted.

"Aiee!" the tracker said softly. "You killed the bear?"

"No, my father did. I tried, and failed."

"You did not fail, my friend. *He* succeeded."

Wolf shook his head. "It does not matter. It is over. Walks in the Sun has said it."

"Ah! You talked to him?"

"Yes. Before he died. It is even now, he said."

"The Covenant? It is made right again?"

"Walks in the Sun has said it."

"Aiee, my friend, your father should know. He was a great holy man."

Wolf said nothing.

"Wolf," Sees went on, "my heart is heavy for you, but I am made to think that the heart of Walks in the Sun was good as he crossed over. Is it not so?"

"Yes, it is as he wished it," Wolf admitted.

"Then our hearts should be good for the People, no? The Covenant is restored. A brave holy man has given his life for the People."

"That is true, Sees. But it will take some time."

"Of course. I will sit with you tonight."

He tossed a couple of sticks on the fire and sat down, drawing his robe around him.

"Thank you, my friend," said Singing Wolf. "It is good."

And so it was. As Walks in the Sun had predicted, it was finally over. The People mourned their holy man, and there were many who understood that in the action he had chosen, the violation of the Covenant had resulted in his own death. After the appropriate period of mourning, the People turned their attention again to the ways of the living. There was no further trouble with bears. It seemed that the holy man had been correct. The Covenant was restored.

In the legends of the Southern band, however, it was remembered for many generations as a time of trouble and ultimate triumph. On the Story Skins, where pictographs retell the history of the People, it is recorded as *The Year of the Bear.* A giant real-bear towers over the figure of a buckskin-clad holy man who boldly attacks with a short spear . . .

GENEALOGY

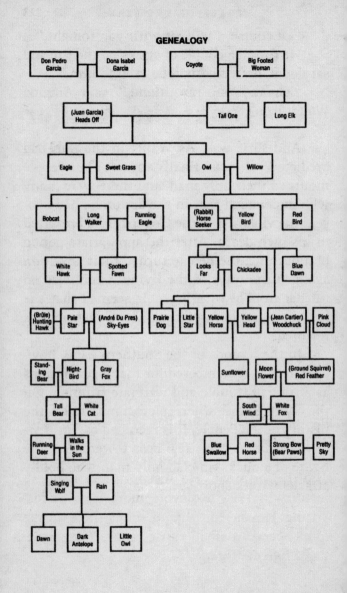

About the Author

» » »

Don Coldsmith was born in Iola, Kansas, in 1926. He served as a World War II combat medic in the South Pacific and returned to his native state, where he graduated from Baker University in 1949 and received his M.D. from the University of Kansas in 1958. He worked at several jobs before entering medical school: he was YMCA Youth Director, a gunsmith, a taxidermist, and for a short time a Congregational preacher. In addition to his private medical practice, Dr. Coldsmith has been a staff physician at the Health Center of Emporia State University, where he also teaches in the English Department. He discontinued medical pursuits in 1990 to devote more time to his writing. He and his wife of thirty-three years, Edna, operate a small cattle ranch. They have raised five daughters.

Dr. Coldsmith produced the first ten novels in the Spanish Bit Saga in a five-year period; he writes and revises the stories first in his head, then in longhand. From this manuscript the final version is skillfully created by his longtime assistant, Ann Bowman.

Of his decision to create, or re-create, the world of the Plains Indian in the early centuries of European contact, the author says: "There has been very little written about this time period. I wanted also to portray these Native Americans as human beings, rather than as stereotyped 'Indians.' As I have researched the time and place, the indigenous cultures, it's been a truly inspiring experience for me. I am not attempting to tell anyone else's story. My only goal is to tell *a* story and tell it fairly."